Something had c   being with her in

On the boat after that, the air had felt physically charged. He could have sworn she felt it too, the way she'd avoided his eyes but couldn't keep hers off his body. The secret thrill had made him ask her here, to something that wasn't work related.

He was regretting it already. The more he found his eyes roving her figure as she followed the shoreline in a long sea green sundress, the more he felt unsettled. She even looked good picking up trash.

He flipped another burger on the grill and served three hungry customers, irritated at the way he couldn't keep his eyes off her, bathed in the final streaks of sunlight. The woman was leaving in a matter of weeks, and even if he did go "there" with tourists, which he absolutely did not, she was working with him. Around Aayla. The last thing he needed was for things to get complicated…

Dear Reader,

Grab your beach towels and a suitable cocktail and get yourself down to the Galápagos Islands. The sun is out, and there's a brooding animal doctor who just can't wait to examine your desires…

If you'd like to join me in supporting the Galapagos Conservation Trust, please head to my website at beckywicks.com for more details. They're working to protect the vulnerable ecosystems found in the Galápagos by conserving species, restoring habitats and fighting climate change.

Becky Wicks

THE VET'S ESCAPE
TO PARADISE

———

BECKY WICKS

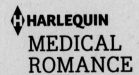

HARLEQUIN
MEDICAL
ROMANCE

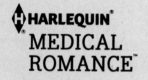

HARLEQUIN®
MEDICAL ROMANCE™

Recycling programs
for this product may
not exist in your area.

ISBN-13: 978-1-335-73737-3

The Vet's Escape to Paradise

Copyright © 2022 by Becky Wicks

For questions and comments about the quality of this book,
please contact us at CustomerService@Harlequin.com.

Harlequin Enterprises ULC
22 Adelaide St. West, 41st Floor
Toronto, Ontario M5H 4E3, Canada
www.Harlequin.com

Printed in U.S.A.

Born in the UK, **Becky Wicks** has suffered interminable wanderlust from an early age. She's lived and worked all over the world, from London to Dubai, Sydney, Bali, New York City and Amsterdam. She's written for the likes of *GQ*, *Hello!*, *Fabulous* and *Time Out*, a host of YA romance, plus three travel memoirs—*Burqalicious*, *Balilicious* and *Latinalicious* (HarperCollins Australia). Now she blends travel with romance for Harlequin and loves every minute! Tweet her @bex_wicks and subscribe at beckywicks.com.

Books by Becky Wicks

Harlequin Medical Romance

Tempted by Her Hot-Shot Doc
From Doctor to Daddy
Enticed by Her Island Billionaire
Falling Again for the Animal Whisperer
Fling with the Children's Heart Doctor
White Christmas with Her Millionaire Doc
A Princess in Naples

Visit the Author Profile page at Harlequin.com.

Dedicated to the Galapagos Conservation Trust, which is working tirelessly to protect the unique species of the islands, restore their natural habitat and provide sustainable solutions for issues like plastic pollution.

Praise for Becky Wicks

"Absolutely entertaining, fast-paced and a story I couldn't put down…. Overall, Ms. Wicks has delivered a wonderful read in this book where the chemistry between this couple was strong; the romance was delightful and special."

—*Harlequin Junkie* on *From Doctor to Daddy*

CHAPTER ONE

'HAVE YOU SEEN any boobies yet?'

Mike snorted a laugh at the end of the phone, all the way from Galway, and Ivy put her feet up on the gilded headboard. Flat on her back on the soft satin sheets of her honeymoon bed, she sighed at the ceiling.

'You just couldn't wait to ask me about the boobies, could you? And yes, they're everywhere if you must know. You can't walk down the street in Santa Cruz without being accosted by a man displaying his rail of *I heart boobies* T-shirts. Even this hotel lobby has a rack of them.'

Boobies were the blue-footed birds she'd been excited to see here in their native home, the Galapagos Islands. Her business partner, Mike, had probably been storing up the question for weeks, waiting till she was actually here on Santa Cruz—the island known as the beating heart of the archipelago—to blurt it out.

'Pick me up a shirt, will you? That would make some of our clients' day!' he said. Then Mike's tone changed. She pictured him pouting the way he did, elbows resting on the reception desk at their veterinary clinic, thin lips pursed in the thick of his grey-flecked beard. 'And how are *you*, Ivy? You're a brave woman, going on your honeymoon to a couples' resort, all by yourself.'

'It just means more chocolates and champagne for *me*,' she said, doing her best to stay chipper, even as the song from *Bridget Jones* popped into her head: 'All by Myself'.

'You forced me to come anyway,' she reminded him, crossing to the balcony. The heat hit her like a hairdryer. She'd given up on taming her mass of red curls in the humidity on day one. Three long days ago. 'You said I needed a holiday.'

'And you do. I don't think you've taken a break since I've known you—you're a thirty-eight-year-old workaholic and you know it. Are you meditating, like I told you to?'

She let Mike impart his limited spiritual knowledge, most of which he usually spouted verbatim from Oprah Winfrey's podcasts, while she let her eyes trail down to the heart-shaped swimming pool. One couple were enjoying the facilities in the fading sunlight, floating their cares away on matchy-matchy inflatable love hearts. Ugh.

It should be her down there with Simon, living the couple's dream. Only Simon was probably three pints deep into another session at The Smuggler's Nook back home, planning new dreams without her.

She'd always hated that pub.

'You'll be glad you both called off the wedding one day,' Mike said, probably reading her thoughts. He had an uncanny knack for it after launching and working at Animal Remedy Referrals at her side for so many years. They knew everything about each other.

'You both agreed you didn't want kids when you met, and he took *this* long to tell you he's changed his mind. You were only dating, what… four and a half years? What else wasn't he telling you?'

'Nothing, Mike,' she said wearily, watching the sickeningly happy couple lean across the gap between their inflatables for a kiss. 'I know you're trying to be a good friend but Simon's a good man, you know it. I know it. We just want different things. Talk to me about the animals. How's Ollie's little pup doing after the parvo scare?'

Mike dutifully changed the subject to their animal patients, while a familiar twinge of anxiety made her clasp her phone tighter. She shouldn't have left them, really. What right did she have to take a honeymoon when she wasn't even married? In South America of all places. She should be home discussing the potential acquisition with Mike. It wasn't every day some huge private equity firm offered you millions to take your business to the next level—or to a whole new set of standards that would match their national portfolio.

Then again, she would have to think about that wherever she was. Mike hadn't said it directly yet, but she knew he was leaning towards selling…even if she was still unsure.

Anyway, this month-long trip had been booked for over a year. It would have been stupid to waste it. October was the best time to be here, coming up to summer in the Southern hemisphere. Besides, her mother had already paid for it…probably out of guilt, she thought. Then she admonished herself for being snarky. Not working right now meant far too much time wrapped up in her own head.

Sure, Simon *could* have informed her of his burning urge to spawn mini-mes before they'd planned the wedding and honeymoon of the century.

But then, maybe he had tried to discuss it.

Maybe she just hadn't been listening. Hadn't wanted to listen.

Sheesh. Being her other half couldn't have been easy. She did like to work. A lot.

Asking Mike to check in with her again tomorrow, just so she could be sure that things were ticking along OK in her absence, and getting a firm 'no way' in response, Ivy wandered down to the pool.

Maybe meditating in the final streaks of sunset would help her relax? If she stayed in her room, she'd just check her work email again and she'd already done that twice today. They laughed about the workaholic thing sometimes, but it wasn't really funny. It hadn't been funny to Simon.

Sometimes the look in her ex's eyes when she'd come home late *again*...even now it made her cringe. She'd done to him what her mother had done to her all those years ago—worked so hard and so late that she'd barely kept track of the time or noticed the emotional effects of her absence on the people around her.

The more she thought about it from a distance, things hadn't exactly been smooth sailing before Simon's grand announcement: *'I think I do want a kid, actually, Ivy. Wouldn't it be grand...a little legacy?'*

She cringed to herself just remembering how

quickly the fear had set in, how quick she'd been to dismiss it: *'I would be a terrible mother, Simon. We both know that.'*

The swimming pool couple were taking cheesy photos in the blue hues of the pool with an underwater camera now. It didn't feel right to intrude; besides, they deserved the couples' pool, being an actual couple.

Ivy veered off the path towards the hotel's private beach, located a sunlounger in the soft white sand and sat cross-legged to meditate.

Deep breath in. Deep breath out. Free the mind, release the ego.

Yeah, right.

With each swoosh of the waves, in swept her ego to chide her.

Children were nice enough, but she didn't exactly know how to relate to them. Most of her own childhood had been spent cooped up in the house with her nanny and her dog, while her mother worked tirelessly, relentlessly, in some office Ivy had only ever visited in her head. Every day after school had been the same after her dad died: she'd been wrapped up in a cocoon, not allowed out to play in case something bad happened to her, too. Pretty soon her friends had stopped calling round altogether.

Thank goodness for Zeus, she thought. That big daft German shepherd had been her whole world. The reason she'd thrown herself into her animal books, then her veterinary studies! Her own career was her baby now. The *reason* she'd chosen a child-free life and future.

She pinged her eyes open, glowering at the horizon over the water.

Why could she not even meditate properly?

Her mind always spun backwards when she didn't keep busy. Oprah would probably give her a right talking-to. How dare she feel even the slightest bit guilty for making her *own* career her baby? She had a big clinic-sized child to nurture and grow as she saw fit. What was so wrong with *that*?

It wasn't as if *she'd* brought an actual child into the world, only to let her other priorities render it invisible.

Ivy bit the insides of her cheeks. It tended to centre the pain somewhere other than her heart. Her dad's death had hit her mother hard, but maybe workaholics ran in the family.

Either way. She wouldn't ever do that; she'd told Simon as much. They'd called everything off seven months ago. All that was left was this non-refundable holiday. Rumour had it he was dating again already.

So now you're alone. Again. Just you. Is that what you really want, Ivy?

Shut up, ego. Breathe in, breathe out...

A frightened squall from the rocks around the water caught her ears and sucker-punched her square in the solar plexus. What the…?

Squinting, she removed herself from her decidedly un-meditational pose and found herself investigating. It sounded like an animal in pain—she'd know that sound anywhere.

'Where are you? *What* are you?'

Navigating around the rocks in her flip-flops, she sent an army of magnificent red Sally Lightfoot crabs scuttling in a scarlet drove away from her.

Sorry, guys, don't mind me.

The Galapagos was no place not to look where you were going; there were more rare species here than anywhere on earth and most of them had a cheerful tolerance of humans, which was exactly why these islands were so special. Already, on her photo expeditions around the island she'd seen more honking sea lions than she could count, and tiptoed around sleepy groups of charcoal marine iguanas, their red underbellies glowing like the embers of a fire. She always thought they looked like little dinosaurs who'd forgotten to become extinct.

It took her less than a minute to locate the source of the noise. She almost reeled, being so close to it. *No way.*

A baby blue-footed booby! Maybe just a

month or so old. For a second, she studied it, in awe of its tiny pale body, light brown wings and distinctively sky-hued webbed feet. Like no other creature on earth.

'Wow,' she gushed, frowning at the deep red gash on its white feathered belly. 'What happened to you?'

The poor thing looked as if it must have got into a fight with one of those marine iguanas that were usually chomping at moss on lava rocks, further up the beach. Both were synonymous with the Galapagos. This was why she'd wanted to come here for as long as she could remember, to witness such native creatures with her own eyes. But seeing one hurt—especially one so young and so small—she wasn't prepared.

'Come here, little buddy, I won't hurt you.'

Careful not to scare it further, she shook off her green T-shirt and scooped it up. Lucky she'd kept her bikini top on underneath. In minutes she was hurrying back up the beach with it.

'I'll…um… I'll have to call Jero.' A stocky, round-faced lady with a name badge reading Nayely had taken one look at the injured bird from behind the reception desk and got on the phone.

Ivy had laid the fledgling out on the pristine

lobby floor on her shirt, much to the interest of the couple who'd come in from the pool. They were standing to her left with their inflatable hearts dripping on the marble tiles, watching her swabbing gently at the wound. Nayely's assistant had located fresh towels and an emergency kit, but it looked as though the wound would need stitches. And probably some kind of special antiseptic. She'd warned them—if it was a bite from an angry iguana, the toxins could kill.

'At least it's still moving, fight or flight going strong,' she said to the crowd as she placed her hand over the bird to keep it still. It wouldn't do to have an injured baby booby flitting erratically about, dropping blood all over their rack of prized booby pun T-shirts.

She was just admiring how its cute little head fitted between her forefinger and her middle finger when a rush of warm air enveloped her. She turned to see a male figure in the revolving doors, and in less than two seconds flat all six-foot-something of the powerfully built man was striding towards her, carrying the scent of the evening and a doctor's bag.

Blinking, she stood to greet him, shocked into silence for a second by his presence. Lean. Athletic. Obviously white Latino, judging by the sun-kissed olive skin stretched over high cheekbones, and charcoal-black hair shaved almost to the scalp, as though he could have walked straight off an army base. He was rocking the hell out of a tight white T-shirt. A wall of muscle flexed in his broad-shouldered back as he said a quick hi and crouched at her feet to inspect the bird.

'Where did you find her?' he asked after a moment, looking up and fixing deep mahogany eyes onto hers. Faint crinkles lined them like parentheses; what was he, thirty-eight like her? Maybe forty?

'On…out there…on the beach.' Ivy cleared her throat, forcing her neurons to fire correctly instead of all over the place. God, he was handsome, and, judging from his accent, American?

'You…work here? On this island, with the animals?' she asked as Nayely appeared again with a cardboard box.

'There's nothing more I can do here; I'll have to take her to the clinic.' He paused, as if remembering her question. 'I'm the founder, head vet and operations manager at the Darwin Animal Clinic,' he replied, diverting his attention back to the bird, which she scooped gently into the box while he held it. She caught the edge of a black tattoo—something jagged and tribal-looking—on his biceps under his shirt.

'That's one hell of a job description,' she said.

'I work with the domestic animals as a rule.

Sometimes we help the Galápagos National Park with injured wildlife, like this. Thank you for getting there first and helping this little one. I'm Jero Morales.'

'Ivy Malone,' she replied, self-consciousness snatching her breath as his bright eyes scanned her up and down from under thick black drawn-together brows. She was shirtless, in just her bikini top. *Doh.* At least she had denim shorts on too and wasn't just standing here directly before him in a two-piece. That would have been awkward because this man was gorgeous.

'Where's the clinic?'

'Not too far from here. We're the only one on Santa Cruz. The only permanent one in the Galapagos.'

'There's only one permanent veterinary clinic, across all the islands?'

'It's more like a shack, but he did start it all from scratch,' Nayely cut in.

Jero's eyebrows raised at the look that must have been on her face. He stood with the box.

'I mean, I just find it hard to believe there's only one,' she continued. 'I'm a vet myself. Back in Ireland.'

He nodded and said something quietly in Spanish to Nayely. The two clearly knew each other—the island was small after all. Ivy found herself wondering where he lived and what else he did on the island when he wasn't caring for sick animals.

Stop swooning, woman!

Suddenly, he was motioning goodbye, and she was speaking without thinking.

'Can I check up on this booby, tomorrow? I'll come by the clinic. Maybe I can even volunteer? I have some time…'

'Sure, Nayely will let you know where I am.' He eyed her up and down again, holding the box against him. She knew instinctively that the bird would be safe in his care. A part of her wanted to *be* that bird.

'I should go,' he said, and she shook herself. What the hell was she doing, crushing out like a schoolgirl?

Must be the heat.

His mouth twitched with a secret smile, and something in her stomach did a backflip as his eyes raked over her torso again. 'Nice to meet you, Ivy,' he said, and she allowed herself the pleasure of watching his pert bottom from behind as he made his way back out into the twilight.

CHAPTER TWO

Ivy WAS STANDING in front of the paper-strewn desk, smelling of coconut sun lotion. She'd come to check on the baby booby, and now she was trying to offer her services. Again.

Jero folded his arms across his navy shirt and put his face into neutral. He was tired after a late night with the school board discussing plans for Aayla's next class outing and his brain was struggling to keep up. So many words, he thought in vague amusement, spilling from Ivy's lips under the whirring air-conditioning unit.

'I have my own veterinary clinic, near Galway. Well, I'm the co-founder of Animal Remedy Referrals. Look it up. My partner, Mike, and I have over forty years of combined experience working in academic institutions and private referral practices. I can show you references. In fact, one client just left a five-star review this morning. There were complications during surgery on her basset hound two weeks ago, but thankfully I—'

'That won't be necessary.'

She pursed her lips as he cut her short. She'd hardly taken a breath till now. Good thing the accent was so interesting. Kind of mesmerising actually. Did she always wear green? Today the T-shirt tucked into her denim shorts was ocean green…or maybe it was Irish-clover green? The one she'd wrapped the booby in had been turquoise and green. Even her bikini was green. He'd appreciated that a lot last night.

She cocked her head and gave him a look that said, *Well?*

'I don't doubt your qualifications, Ivy, but we don't have any paid positions right now.'

'Payment?' She looked affronted. 'You think I'm here looking for a job? I just told you, Jero, I have my own clinic in Galway. Although I've recently contemplated selling, if you must know; there's talk of an acquisition by a private-equity-backed group, Blue Stream Veterinary Alliance?'

She paused as if he might have heard of it, which of course he hadn't. 'They're very impressed with our…' She trailed off, maybe sensing his amusement.

'Anyway. I'm here on my honeymoon.' Her eyes darted sideways. 'Kind of.'

He felt his eyebrows arc to his hairline. Now, this was interesting. *Kind of?*

'I'm just offering my help while I'm here. It's what I do. You have other volunteers, don't you?'

He perched on the edge of the table, folding his arms again and catching her trace his tattoo with her eyes. 'Why would you want to volunteer here while you're on your honeymoon? Wouldn't that cut into your cocktail-sipping, scuba-diving agenda?'

Ivy's amber eyes drew a line up from his tattoo to his face. When they locked onto his he wondered how she'd stuck a hummingbird in place of his heart already. She'd done it yesterday too, in the hotel lobby, the second she'd looked up at him with that booby fledgling in her hands.

He dragged a hand along his chin, trying not to linger in her stare, or let his eyes drop to her shapely legs in those shorts. Ivy Malone was something to look at with that sharp, diminutive chin and angular cheekbones, and breasts like two squeezable peaches in a green bikini.

She was married, he reminded himself. On her honeymoon.

'I'm pretty sure your husband wants you with him at any rate; hotels like the one you guys are in cost a fortune,' he said. 'If I were you, I'd be horizontal on a sunbed...'

He stopped talking. That might have come out wrong; he'd been distracted.

'My husband's not here.' Ivy swiped her fingertip across a photo of his team, taken six months ago on turtle release day, then swiped the dust off onto her jean shorts. He cringed inside. The reception area wasn't exactly spotless today. *Or any day.*

'I don't have a husband.' She paused. 'Not even a fiancé any more.'

'I'm confused.' Jero rubbed his arms, blindsided. The Aqua Breeze Couples' Resort was famous for honeymooners and…well…couples.

'Don't be. It's really very clear. I have spare time, and you look like you could do with some help around here.'

She motioned with her eyes to the mountain of paperwork on the desk, and the Manila files poking haphazardly from the cardboard boxes on the shelving unit by the wall. He prayed the posters wouldn't start drooping under her scrutiny.

The surgery and storage rooms were spotless, of course, someone cleaned those every day, meticulously, which was why no one had time to sort the reception area out—they were too busy. Always. It was one thing after the other and his team of volunteers were already all in a million places at once.

But that wasn't all he was thinking now. This woman needed a distraction from whatever had happened with her…fiancé?

What went down there? A woman honeymooning alone at the island's top five-star couples-only resort was not exactly an everyday occurrence. Was she a jilted bride, maybe?

What if her would-be husband had dropped dead or something? He'd heard a story like that once from a chambermaid at The Spotted Finch Hotel in town. Some guy had a heart attack the night of the wedding and left his wife of less than eight hours a widow.

A widow at Ivy's age; what was she, mid-thirties? That would be even worse than what had happened to him and Aayla, which the whole island agreed, mostly behind his and his daughter's back, was pretty terrible.

'Just think about it?' she pushed, digging into her denim pocket and producing a business card. He turned it over in his hand, feeling his lips twitch at the cliched pawprint logo above the web address. 'Look me up. I think you'll find I'm legitimate.'

'I have no doubt,' he heard himself say, studying the slightly crumpled card. *Ivy Malone.* It sounded like a song in his brain. He found himself scrubbing a hand through where his hair used to be. He'd shaved it a week ago. It was getting too damn hot again already.

'I'll be waiting to hear from you, then,' she said. Ivy turned to leave, but swung back at the last second, picking up a book that was threatening to fall from the low-level table by the door—one of many Spanish- and English-language books he kept here for Aayla. She was fluent in both.

'I used to love this book!'

Opening it at the centre, Ivy traced a finger over the hungry caterpillar, and her face lit up like sunshine. 'Ooh, it's in Spanish, of course. I wonder if it's the same as I remember it in English. I used to read this to my dog, Zeus.'

'Really?'

Her eyes narrowed. 'Zeus appreciated it when I read to him.'

'It was one of my favourites, too,' he said, noticing the dust-free streak her finger had left on the team photo—he really should dust it all off. In fact, he was going to do that the second she left. 'I kept it for my daughter—she's six, and now *she* loves it, maybe more than I ever did.'

'Oh, yes, you have a daughter. Nayely from the hotel did mention that.'

He bristled. So, she'd heard the story too, then. Nayely had probably recounted it all when he'd left the lobby, whether Ivy had asked her about him or not. Single father, born in Quito, raised in Texas, moved to the Galapagos eight years ago, married a tourist he assumed, wrongly, wanted what he did—the happy family, the life they went on to build—who then went on to ditch him for another tourist. A corporate overlord from Washington DC, no less. All of which left him raising their 'wild', 'feral' island child here alone.

He'd had various exaggerated accounts of it relayed to him over the years. No one could keep anything to themselves around here.

Ivy flicked through the pages, bobbing her head of curls as if reliving her own childhood memories. 'You can borrow it if you want,' he heard himself say, just as he noticed she didn't look happy in this moment of nostalgia any more.

She frowned. 'I'll leave it with you. Just in case we don't actually see each other again.'

'Retracting your offer to volunteer for me, now that you've seen the state of this place?'

'Is that what you want?' She placed the book back on the table slowly and he kicked himself for highlighting the mess.

'Not necessarily,' he added quickly. The state of things at the clinic had nothing to do with why she wouldn't take the book, he could tell that much by the look on her face. Not that he had time to read into it. He could see a call-out coming in as they spoke.

Ivy forced another smile in his direction. 'Well, thanks for letting me check on the booby, Jero. Do let me know if you need me,' she said on her way out.

Jero thought about Ivy most of the afternoon, and the morning after that as he made his way to the fish market. Maybe he should just let her work with him. He sure needed her.

But maybe he shouldn't.

Why the hell did accepting help from anyone he hadn't personally invited into his orbit still get old wounds stinging?

His trust issues caused him to cut off his own nose to spite his face sometimes, but the way she'd told him how he clearly needed some help…that still stung.

He should be able to juggle everything by now; it shouldn't matter one iota that he was raising Aayla on his own and running the island's only veterinary clinic, as well as a hundred other projects. He should be able to stay on top of his work *and* provide everything she needed. Millions of people got divorced and made it work. Everything should be under control and on his own terms by now: his life, his home, his work.

Except it wasn't.

Yolanda, the National Park vet, was still off raising funds for a new project on the mainland. Zenon, who'd been on Guayaquil time since his arrival six months ago, had taken a second sick day in a row.

Dudders—short for Daniel Dudley—his well-meaning import from Britain via a gap year at a monkey sanctuary in Thailand, had turned up an hour late again, albeit dragging a crate of overdue dog food he'd lugged all the way from the ferry port.

Things were always late. So were people. He needed another pair of hands; someone he could count on. Hailey, the first full-time surgeon he'd managed to keep for longer than a year, was still in New Zealand, nursing her sick father. He really should advertise the position again, but she'd begged him not to. She wanted to return. She just didn't know when she could.

The sterilisation programme they'd started called him all over the place. No one with an unsterilised dog was refused, which meant he'd put out a mobile service to the other inhabited islands too—Isabela, San Cristobal, and Floreana.

It was against Galapagos laws to transport any animals between islands. Cross-contamination was a big deal; they had to go to them. Cats and dogs carried diseases and parasites that affected the endemic wildlife. The result was sadly much animal neglect, homelessness and overpopulation. If *they* didn't keep it under control, more local wildlife would suffer. It was all hands on deck, *without* all the other work on top...

'Fancy seeing you here.' A familiar Irish voice stopped him in his tracks. Ivy's eyes fell to where Aayla was standing at his side five metres from the port, where the Puerto Ayora fish market was as loud and smelly as ever. Her small hand clutched his tighter as she slurped the last dregs from a carton of orange juice.

'Oh...hi...you.' Ivy looked and sounded kind of uncomfortable.

Aayla swallowed loudly. 'Hi,' she echoed, eyeing her in interest from under her sunhat. 'I like your camera.'

'Er... Thanks.' Ivy refocused on him, squared her slender shoulders. 'So, you didn't call.'

Awkward.

He pulled his sunglasses off his face and... damn, she was striking in the blazing sunlight. The breeze blew in across the crowds and the port and tussled with her red curls; the colour of flames in a wildfire, he thought, watching them lick her shoulder blades.

She was still wearing the shorts, this time with a skimpy white cotton vest top tucked in behind the camera hanging around her neck.

No green…except for the headband and dangly emerald earrings. Her shapely legs went on for ever before they hit the flip-flops on her feet. Her pale milky skin was a little red around the bikini straps, not that he should be looking.

'I was going to get in touch. I've just been…'

'Busy?' she finished, just as a sea lion's bellow from behind her made her jump and almost land in his arms.

Aayla giggled. 'That's just Álvaro. He's not scary!'

Aayla was used to things like this. Flapping giant wings, swishing tails like swords and wildlife honking louder than a city-centre traffic jam were normal to most people round here. Obviously they weren't to Ivy. A crowd of locals lining up for their fish sniggered at her 'tourist' reaction. Álvaro—a fish market resident who probably weighed as much as a small elephant—was laughing too; at least it seemed as if he was laughing. Ivy broke contact from where her hand had landed on his other arm.

'Sorry,' she said, flustered, before catching his gaze and holding it.

'Aayla, go see Marsha over there,' he instructed, still glued to her eyes.

Ivy was irrefutably attractive. But *that* look in her eyes…that was it. That was what had rattled the cage he sometimes forgot his heart was all locked up in.

He hadn't felt a pull like this to anyone in a long time. He'd probably, on some subconscious level, turned a blind eye to his needs in *that* department since Mitch, the Washington overlord, sailed up to the island and left seven months later having fully secured Jero's wife for himself. He still couldn't say Suranne's name out loud without it burning like a bad tattoo. She was meant to call Aayla last Sunday. She still hadn't bothered.

'Daddy! Over here!' Aayla was waving at him profusely from Marsha's table, covered with crates of iced yellowfin tuna, groupers and red snapper. 'Daddy, there are seven of them!'

'Seven of what?' Ivy looked primed for involvement in whatever Aayla was talking about now.

Looks like this woman isn't going anywhere.

With a heavy sigh under his breath, he beckoned her with him as he stepped over Álvaro, and a pelican promptly tried to land on his shoulder. Waving it off gently, he led her to Marsha's market stall, where Aayla was already on bended knees, lifting the plastic sheet up and peering into a box on the concrete floor.

'Found them this morning,' Marsha said, stepping around his daughter to hand a paper parcel of hot-pink scorpion fish over to a customer. 'Figured you were the man to call. Didn't have time to drop them off before I had to be here.'

'You did the right thing,' he said. Marsha was like a mother to him, and most people on the island. Her stall at the fish market had been manned—or womanned, as she liked to say— for the last four generations and this sea lion had become somewhat of her surrogate son.

'They're probably only three, maybe four weeks old,' Ivy said as they both dropped beside Aayla to inspect the puppies. Each one was a slightly different colour, their ears still pink and floppy, wriggling and writhing around on top of each other.

'Any sign of the mother?' he asked Marsha. Then he realised Ivy had said the exact same thing in harmony.

'You're funny.' Aayla giggled. 'I like your camera.'

Ivy suppressed a smile. 'You already said that.'

Aayla looked up at her beseechingly. 'Can I take some photos of them?'

'Not now.'

Ivy stepped away as he pulled the cardboard box of puppies out and Marsha swept a fish head off her table of fresh catch, narrowly missing Ivy's head. Álvaro waddled up for his prize. Just then, a battle commenced between him and the pelican in a showdown of wings, squawks and honks, but Ivy wasn't even looking now. Her amber eyes stayed fixed on the pups as he placed them on a nearby empty table. One by one she helped him check them over, while the tourists looked on in interest. No visible signs of injury. But Marsha hadn't seen the mother either.

'We'll get them to the clinic. They'll need de-worming asap,' he told her. 'Then I guess we add them to the adoption register.'

Ivy raised an eyebrow. 'We. Does that mean you want me on your team?'

Now it was his turn to suppress a smile.

Her qualifications were undeniably impressive. He himself had internal medicine and emergencies covered, but Ivy was a licensed orthopaedic surgeon with countless other creds in animal care. From what he'd seen online, aside from the Doctor of Veterinary Medicine, she had more testimonials and glowing accolades and award-winning papers under her belt than anyone he'd ever met. It looked as if she hadn't done anything but work since she graduated vet school…if anything she was overqualified, but she did seem enthusiastic.

Or she wants to distract herself on her solo honeymoon. What the hell happened there?

Why did he even care? He needed help at the

clinic, and help was what he'd got, of literally the highest degree.

'Can I take some photos now?' Aayla asked as they made their way back to his car. She made a grab for the camera, and he told her to watch her manners. Aayla pouted. Ivy looked unsure, but eventually she unhooked it from around her neck and handed it over, which made him smile.

'You have to look through here,' she explained, stopping on the dusty palm-lined path to the road to lean over his curious daughter's slight, six-year-old frame and show her the view-finder.

Something in him shifted as her bright red curls meshed with his daughter's volcano-black locks for just a second. If only he could get a photo from where *he* was standing, but his arms were full of puppies. Aayla had never held a real camera before.

'Don't drop it,' Ivy pleaded.

Aayla tutted. 'Why would I drop it?'

The two of them bantered all the way back to the clinic, in the back seat with the puppies. He listened in, fighting back the odd laugh. Ivy probed him on his role, work, the clinic, the sterilisation programme, while Aayla probed *her* on how to use the camera.

From Ivy's short, not cold, but slightly awkward answers to all of Aayla's questions he got the impression that she hadn't spent much time around kids. At times she spoke like some kind of robot: forced, mechanical. Aayla just found her more amusing for it.

'You're good with her,' he told her later, when they'd settled the pups into their cage in the back room, now thankfully wormed and vaccinated. Seven less domestics to worry about—they'd be put up for adoption as soon as Dudders got back from wherever he was now and entered them into the system. That was his role.

One of them anyway. Dudders had many roles, they all did.

'Did you hear me? I said Aayla seems to like you,' he said again, when he realised she hadn't responded.

He was surprised that a compliment regarding a stranger with Aayla came so easily out of his mouth when normally it would take ages to even think that about a new person. But from her trepidation he sensed it was something Ivy might need to hear. Anyway, Ivy Malone was going to have to get used to Aayla if she was going to be hanging around the clinic, he thought. It was basically the kid's second home, when she wasn't at school or with Nina, her nanny.

'I'm really *not* good with kids,' she replied now, crouching over their little booby fledgling.

Aayla had named her already—Pluma, which meant 'feather'.

Jero peered around the door, where Aayla was colouring in a picture book of cats at the little table. 'She's never held a real camera before. Not till you showed her yours,' he told her.

Ivy curled her fingers round the bird's cage, peering inside. Her face got lost behind her mass of red hair. 'I know cameras, that's all. Cameras and animals.'

There was a sadness to her tone again, and he didn't know what to say. Pluma was cooing in her own little cage under the Darwin quote poster, which read: *The love for all living creatures is the most noble attribute of man.* Hailey had scribbled out *man* and replaced it with *woman*, and he was just about to comment on it, to break the awkward silence, when Aayla bounced back in and asked if she could help Ivy feed worms to Pluma, then take more photos.

He shifted a pile of unattended paperwork to locate the worms and tried to ignore the look Ivy shot him. Yes, OK, the place could be a little more organised, he'd been meaning to address that, but calls were coming in already. A tortoise with a cracked shell and flesh wound over on Floreana that he'd have to see to onsite, thanks to Yolanda being off-island. A pregnant dog had also just been found in a rubbish container.

He answered a call from Zenon, who'd finally woken up from his siesta, watching Ivy and Aayla interact around Pluma the whole time.

Poor little Pluma had probably been abandoned by her mother after being attacked, he thought, trying to ignore the way he couldn't stop wondering things about Ivy. She was here to work, that was all, and she was under no obligation to tell him anything else about herself. Just because she'd probably heard everything about him, from the island gossips, didn't mean it was his place to ask what happened with her ex, or why she was honeymooning alone. Or why she assumed she'd never been any good with kids.

She was reserved around his daughter, sure, but a little less awkward now than when they'd first met, a couple of hours ago.

'Look, Ivy, Pluma just lifted her head up!'

'You're right, she did. She's getting stronger already.'

Despite her insistence on being no good with kids, if it carried on like this, the two might actually form some kind of friendship, he thought to himself absently. Aayla was pretty addictive, but maybe he was biased.

Ivy would be out and about all the time, with him more than Aayla—if she wanted to work, he'd give her work. Besides, tourists never stuck around too long anyway.

Especially unmarried, single, highly qualified, strikingly beautiful ones...

Good thing too, he thought suddenly, catching himself. He'd have to start making sure they didn't bond, for Aayla's sake.

There was absolutely no way he'd have his daughter's heart broken by anyone *else* filling her head with possibilities, and then walking out of her world.

CHAPTER THREE

IVY FLATTENED A hand to her hair. The salty ocean breeze was going to leave it looking wilder than ever after this boat ride. She wouldn't care if she weren't with Jero but she'd caught him looking at her as if she were some kind of entertaining alien over the past few days and it was making her self-conscious.

They'd been talking about climate change. How the United Nations reported up to thirty per cent of plant and animal species around the world were at risk of extinction. 'I know islands like this are especially vulnerable,' she said now, over the sound of the engine.

Jero bobbed his shaved head towards the island ahead. The boat was speeding towards Floreana, where a café owner had called concerned about a mystery wound on his dog's hind leg.

'Why do you think I stay out here?' he said. 'There's more work to do than you even know.'

Ivy pursed her lips, training her eyes on the

slope of his nose. The sun was reflecting the ocean spray in his sunglasses, hiding those dreamy eyes. OK, she might have told a little white lie to Mike this morning when she said she didn't find her new Galapagos mentor hot, but it wasn't for a man, or anyone, to tell her what she knew.

Then again, he had a point. What did she know? This was her first visit to the Galapagos after all.

'So…how long have you been out here?' she asked, watching the pier draw closer. The midday sun was already scorching her bare arms through her sunscreen; this place was still a shock to her Irish skin. 'I'm guessing you weren't born in the Galapagos Islands, like Aayla was?'

His dark brows drew together. 'Nope. My parents raised me a Galveston boy. We lived one mile from the beach…in fact I haven't lived that far away from it since.'

Ah, that was right, Texas, she thought, remembering what the receptionist at the hotel had said.

Jero tossed the buffers over the side of the boat, and she pretended not to notice how his sunscreened olive biceps glistened like a rock under his black tattoo. Simon hadn't had a bad physique, but he'd been nowhere near as muscular or toned. She wondered, would the magic have lasted longer if he had been more physically attractive, instead of kind, attentive and… safe?

Was there ever really any magic to begin with?

Ivy frowned to herself. Sometimes she had to think really hard about that. Maybe she'd wanted the magic so much that she'd merely convinced herself that she and Simon had it.

In truth, her heart had never really had to heal from Simon, because it hadn't been all that broken by the break-up. She hadn't ever admitted that to anyone—it was hard enough to admit it to herself, let alone everyone else. Her friends all seemed to expect a crumpled mess in her company after it all fell apart. So how could she admit that she'd spent over four long years with someone who, through no real fault of his own, had failed to make her feel the way she truly *wanted* to feel about a partner, a husband? That she'd been waiting for the sparks to suddenly ignite?

She always knew they wouldn't. But safety and security meant more than physical attraction and chemistry. Those things were more important. Those were the things she *needed*.

At least, that was what she'd told herself after the string of man-children she'd met online,

who'd disappeared after just one date. Maybe
she'd given up, after that. It wasn't something
she enjoyed thinking about, but maybe she'd
'settled' with Simon out of fear she'd never
meet anyone she really connected with. The kids
thing had been a convenient excuse to get out of
it, really, in the end. A wake-up call.

What was Jero's tattoo of? She studied it
again, while he bantered with the driver in Spanish, and tried to shove Simon from her head.

God, it was sexy hearing Jero speak Spanish.
She spoke a little herself, but the two spoke so
fast she could barely keep up. It bothered her,
feeling left out, no thanks to spending the majority of her formative years all by herself. Well,
apart from the nanny.

Maybe it bothered her more because she liked
Jero more than she wanted to already, more than
was safe to, considering her temporary status
here. Best to keep it professional, she decided. A
'look but don't touch' kind of thing. It wouldn't
be hard. Aside from his looks, he was still somewhat a mystery.

She knew about his work obviously. And how
his full-time surgeon Hailey, had left for New
Zealand, leaving him with a team of volunteers
who weren't always the most reliable. She'd seen
them do things around the clinic that they certainly wouldn't be doing if they worked for *her*.

But he was doing immeasurable good around the islands. Late last year they'd managed to acquire a new licence and had sterilised almost two thousand animals. They'd worked hard to eradicate the threat of parvovirus and stop distemper reaching the Galapagos sea lion population.

Jero had explained how he'd started leading outreach events and doing school talks too. Most people thought the thousands of dogs on the four inhabited islands were harmless. But he'd stressed to her how they were very much invasive animals, who harassed and preyed on the finches and marine and land iguanas, the birds and, Aayla's favourites, the young giant tortoises. It was nothing short of inspiring, how he wanted to educate people and train even more Galapagos community members and give them the tools to secure a sustainable future. All of this was as important to Jero as raising Aayla.

Well, almost.

It was obvious that Jero loved that little girl like nothing else. Aayla Morales *was* pretty cute, Ivy thought now, all big brown, bright joyous eyes, and raven-black hair with a glossy sheen she'd have killed for as a kid. She had crazy curls, and rosy cheeks you just wanted to squeeze. Watching them together made Ivy forget herself sometimes; she just wished she were

as good with her as Jero seemed to think she
was. Obviously he only said that stuff to be nice.

She swallowed back the bitter taste that always came when she was reminded, in any way,
of how bad she was with kids. Even though
Simon had argued it was all in her head. He'd
said she was calling herself 'unsuitable' and
them 'noisy' or 'expensive' or 'time-consum-
ing' as excuses to not have them herself, because she was afraid she'd be a bad mother, as
her own was.

Maybe he was half right. Or maybe she just
didn't want to go there with *him*.

Ugh.

It didn't matter, she was only here for another
couple of weeks. She might as well use her experience to be of use. And learn something too.
What else was she supposed to do?

'Relax!' Mike had almost yelled at her this
morning, after he'd wound her up unknow-
ingly by mentioning the acquisition again. Blue
Stream Veterinary Alliance were coming down
hard now, upping their offer, not just for the cen-
tral location in Galway, but for the reputation
they'd spent years building. It meant freedom
for her and Mike, to cast their nets wider somewhere else, or to just enjoy a small fortune, but
this was her baby!

She was trying not to think about it here; although, if she was honest, this *was* one of the reasons she'd come away. To think. Money wasn't everything.

'Experiences like this are better for my mental health,' she'd told him anyway. *'It's invaluable really.'*

He'd asked if it had anything to do with Jero—he'd looked him up, apparently, called him 'her type', as if she had a type. She'd told him absolutely not.

A big, fat, not-so-little white lie.

Jero was very easy on the eye. Even when the state of the Darwin Animal Clinic gave her heart palpitations, just looking at him made it less relevant somehow.

That place was far from organised. Volunteers were expected to work five days a week and help with being on call on weekends, on a shared rota. They worked seven-thirty a.m. to eleven-thirty a.m., closed for a long siesta, which everyone took but herself and Jero, then reopened in the late afternoon once the temperature had dropped. Sometimes they worked till seven-thirty p.m.

Typically, surgeries including spaying and neutering were performed in the morning, and most walk-in consultations or off-island calls were in the afternoon. No one was fully responsible for filing the paperwork in those ridiculously outdated Manila folders, as far as she could tell. Everyone did their bit, or at least they were supposed to.

She was itching to reorganise. Practically chomping at the bit already, but no.

It wasn't her place to get involved in any of that. She could get bossy and she knew it. Things were different here; they were also working with far less than adequate equipment. But yikes! How anyone could work like that for long was a mystery to her.

'So, what brought you over here?' she asked Jero, realising she'd been watching him, watching the waves, reorganising his life in her head.

'I moved back to Quito to study.'

'Back to?'

'I was born in Ecuador. It was Dad's job that took us to Texas, but I guess I never felt like I belonged there. I opened the clinic on Santa Cruz a couple years before Aayla came along; it was just a shack then. Grew it out from there, had our own place built in town. Home is home, you know? I think your heart knows, anyway.'

Ivy nodded thoughtfully. Her heart had never known anything but Ireland. Was she boring? Gosh, maybe he thought her so. Her pride went down a notch on the spot.

Jero finished swigging from a bottle of water, kicked a foot up on the bench opposite her and gripped the mast with one big hand as they bumped over a wave. 'My ex-wife, she's American. Met her right here. She was on vacation. Never thought I'd marry a tourist but...'

'Your heart knows, right?'

Jero tossed the water bottle into a crate and huffed a laugh that made her kick herself. 'Never thought I'd divorce one either. But we had Aayla. So, I must have done something right.'

She pulled a face. He was divorced, of course, why had she just said that? Why was he making her nervous?

He grabbed up the bag of supplies they'd brought, and she followed him to the front of the boat, where the driver, Nico, hosed their feet, hands and legs down while a big fat sea lion eyed them sleepily from one of the benches by the pier.

It was still weird, this washing process. Jero said it was to eliminate any bacteria and prevent contamination between the islands.

They walked in silence along the sandy cobblestone road towards the café. His butt looked like two more rocks, and she couldn't help wondering if it was as hard as it looked in those black shorts. Was he still single?

She couldn't help but hope he was, even though it didn't matter in the slightest really. Dating a father meant the child came along with him, and for multiple reasons she was definitely not what either of them needed.

Jero was a man of few words when it came to his private life, but his unsettled state about his ex had been more than clear in his clipped tone back on the boat. She did already know *some* of his story. All she'd done was ask Nayely if he'd lived on the island long—out of interest, because he was a vet too, not because visions of his buff body and piercing eyes had struck her like a gamma ray at first sight.

Nayely had told her the whole story. Her version anyway, right after he'd left the lobby. He'd married some younger woman, a tourist. Bit of a whirlwind situation, apparently. Aayla was a mistake, but he'd loved her mother madly; Aayla too when she came along. Then, a few years later his wife wound up cheating on him with some other American guy who'd been visiting the island. She and this new guy lived in Washington DC now. They had another kid and she hardly ever called Aayla. Jero was raising their daughter alone…with a nanny, whom Ivy hadn't met yet.

Aayla was always either at school, where she was now, or in the clinic, trailing *her*, asking if she could use her camera.

Annoying.

Well…not annoying, Ivy caught herself. That

was unfair; she was just being a kid. She was more annoyed at herself for never knowing how to act around her. Of course it must show. At least they had little Pluma and the puppies to care for together. Aayla loved that little booby bird; she'd taken some pretty good photos of her too, so far. OK, a few blurry ones also, but the girl was a good listener, picked things up fast. Maybe Ivy should let her use the camera more often, she considered, under strict supervision, of course.

'What are you smiling at?' Jero opened the door to the run-down shack that constituted a café and her stomach performed a little flip at the look on his face.

'What do you mean?'

'You were smiling, ear to ear.'

'Was I?' she said.

Well, look at that. She actually had been.

Luckily the middle-aged island local in the road-side café near the beach just needed an introduction to some of Jero's antibiotic ointment. Ivy covered the wound on the simpering dog's hind leg with a sterile gauze pad and told the portly man in a vest top not to let the dog lick the affected area.

'We need a cone, really,' she told Jero, touching his arm lightly, registering how the heat of him did something to her insides instantly.

'We don't use them—they create too much plastic waste,' he said, swiping a hand across his forehead.

'How did it happen?' she asked the rotund man in the vest. He was sipping from a can of beer with his feet up on a stack of cardboard boxes in the storage room, watching them kneel on the floor in the hot, stuffy room beside his dog. He said he didn't know, which left Ivy more concerned than she thought best to show.

'People don't always treat their animals here like they do in the west,' Jero told her, on their way back out into the sunshine. It was late afternoon now, and she was tired from the long day attending to calls like this.

'I was starting to get that impression.'

'They just let them wander around, or chain them up as guard dogs. At least we got him to bring him to the mobile clinic next week, when we come back to sterilise.'

We. There it was again. She followed him back up the dusty path. It was nice that he was starting to see her as a real valuable team member, and the word sounded inclusive on a level that lifted her heart for a second...but she did have a flight home booked in two weeks' time.

'Wait.' Jero put an arm out. Ivy stopped in

her tracks. She sucked in a breath at the almost-contact. 'Look,' he said, and she followed his eyes to the sea beyond the bushes and the tiny beach ahead, framed by dark lava rocks and palo santo trees.

'What is it?' She was intrigued now by the sight of the water. It looked as if a set of special waves were erupting in a current of their own. Jero sprinted across the road to the beach, dropped the bag to the sand and started fishing masks and snorkels out of it quickly. Another sea lion and its calf watched them from the shoreline, then waddled into the water as she reached him.

'This is rare to see from the beach, if it is what I think it is!' His enthusiasm was so infectious she laughed. 'You don't want to miss this,' he said, and swiftly pulled his shirt over his head. She almost staggered backwards. His ripped torso totally tore her eyes from the weird commotion in the water.

Wow.

Was he going to pull his shorts off too?

Nope. He made a hurry-up movement with his hand.

'OK, OK!' Stripping down to her bikini, she didn't even have time to feel self-conscious, even when he fixed the mask over her head and pulled at the straps, being careful not to pull her hair.

'How does that feel?' His deep chocolate eyes searched hers and her brain went blank. His body was everything she'd expected, and his breath turned her insides to fire. It, mingled with his suntan lotion, created an inexplicably delicious tang.

'It feels good,' she managed, and he smiled with one side of his mouth, then shook his head, as if he was battling something he wanted to say all of a sudden. Apprehension pooled in her belly. Then he motioned her into the water.

In seconds his strong arms were carving through the turquoise shallows with her close behind. A green sea turtle gave her the eye from the seabed, but still he pressed on. She had no clue what they were even aiming for... Until she saw it.

The giant manta ray stole all the breath from her lungs as she stopped just short of ploughing into Jero in the water. He grinned around his snorkel as her eyes grew wide. The creature was as huge as a silver satellite dish, gracefully gliding through the blue with no apparent fear of their proximity. Inches from her mask, it was overwhelming to see, but then it performed some kind of spinning move, spiralling up to the surface, sending her and Jero to the surface with it.

'They breach like this, to get the parasites

off their undersides,' he explained, pulling his mask and snorkel down to his neck. He found her hand and she gasped, tasting salt at the back of her throat. His brow furrowed as he drew her closer. 'Are you OK?'

She was trying not to show it, because the spectacle was incredible, but they'd swum a little too far out than she was really comfortable with. 'I'm OK. That was…beautiful.' She laughed softly, knowing her nervousness escaped with it.

'You're a good swimmer, aren't you? I didn't even ask.' Jero trod water, right up close; so close his billowing shorts tickled her hipbones and sent a different kind of current rippling through her insides. She studied the droplets of water on his thick black eyelashes as he took her shoulders with firm reassuring hands. The whole ocean seemed to close in around them.

'I followed you out here, didn't I?' confusion made her snap before she swam away from him on her back.

Distance was imperative, before she lost her mind completely. What the heck was that? She'd almost wanted to pull him close, to feel those muscles pressed against her. The way he'd been looking at her; she knew that look. He might not have pushed her away but no…no way.

The guy wasn't in it for some silly fling with a volunteer and she certainly wasn't here for that either. Especially not with a single dad. Her libido was too fired up; she'd been single for the majority of the year, and since she'd got here to the Galapagos she'd been a permanent odd one out around all those mushy couples at the hotel. He probably hadn't felt half of what she'd just felt; it was all in her head. He was merely concerned she might drown.

Jero was already underwater, diving back down to the manta. Reluctantly she followed him back down into the blue, mind reeling. But as soon as she was under, a sense of calm enveloped her and stuck, even when she was forced up for air. The sight of Jero circling the manta as it drifted silently around the coral like a silver spaceship was as mesmerising as the creature itself.

Suddenly, another one appeared from the blue. Then another, until there were five. The commanding creatures were hypnotising, dancing like a synchronised swimming team. Wow. Maybe *this* was how she meditated, from now on.

Back on the beach Ivy got her first glimpse of Jero's full tattoo up close. It wasn't a dragon, as she'd thought from past stolen glimpses. It was actually a giant manta like the one they'd just seen, swimming at an angle, drawn from jet-black blocks of what looked like Mayan symbols.

Sexy as hell on his tanned upper arm.

He caught her looking at it as he stuffed the snorkels back into his bag, and she couldn't divert her eyes fast enough.

'When did you get that?' she asked, to mask the fact that she was now entirely too self-conscious of her wet white shirt over her bikini. He shrugged back into his shirt, swiped a hand over his head and slung the bag back over the other shoulder. Then he pulled up his sleeve again, revealing the tattoo to her, like an art piece he'd spent hours sculpting, as he obviously had his arm.

'I got it after my first visit here, when I came to see if I could really live here.'

She cleared her throat. 'Nice,' she said, wondering if he could tell how he was making her feel, getting half naked and showing her the wonders of the deep. How dared he? Now she wanted to do it again. 'What does it mean?'

He cocked an eyebrow, pulled his sleeve back down. 'It means I got a tattoo.'

'Yes, but all those symbols.'

'Do they have to have a meaning?'

She rolled her eyes but couldn't help match his smile as he led her back to the road and made for the boat.

* * *

'I want to snorkel again,' she said when they were bumping their way back across to Santa Cruz. Jero laughed behind his sunglasses, a foot away from her on the bench.

'You're in the right place. I think your hotel runs snorkelling trips, right?'

She frowned at the horizon. 'Yeah, right. Me and a bunch of couples. Sounds like a blast.'

Jero ran a hand along his jaw, and she felt her face redden. She hadn't meant to imply she was resentful or have him worry about her for any reason. 'I mean, I'd much rather spend my time with you…volunteering. For the next two weeks. I'm learning a lot. And that's something I don't say often to strangers.'

'I'm a stranger, am I?' He smirked into his shoulder, and she gripped the mast, feeling herself sliding towards him with the motion of the boat; or the undeniable chemistry she could feel intensifying by the second. Unless she was imagining it? She still couldn't decide, but, really, why would someone like Jero want anything more than her skill set?

'Funny you think that,' he said. 'You know more about me than I know about you.'

She squared her shoulders. He had a point. She hadn't exactly spilled her heart to her newly appointed mentor about Simon, or the break-up, or the reasons behind it. Jero was a father; one who was raising his daughter alone. Besides, he'd never asked her much about herself anyway.

'All by yourself at the Aqua Breeze,' he continued now, making her heart tangle up in her ribs. He reached for two more bottles of water, passed one to her, eyeing her almost cautiously. 'What are you doing tonight?'

Her head sprang up to meet his eyes. She had a date with a treatment and nutrition plan for Mrs O'Brian's senior cocker spaniel back in Galway, which she'd insisted on helping with from afar, much to Mike's very vocal chagrin. 'I did have a plan...'

'Cancel it. There's a beach clean-up we do every week. I usually man the barbecue afterwards for the volunteers. It's a fun time, you should join us.'

Ivy looked to her feet, feeling his eyes still roving her profile. Butterflies fluttered a trail around her navel. 'I'll think about it. Thank you.'

He nodded and took a swig from the bottle that showcased his Adam's apple and his biceps from a whole new intoxicating angle. She resisted the urge to say she'd come.

She probably shouldn't.

She should be gunning the butterflies down one by one, right as they took flight. It would be a very good idea to stay away from all non-work-related events with Jero; picturing him naked when they were supposed to be saving lives together was not conducive to a productive learning environment. If only she could forget this unfortunate, futile crush.

CHAPTER FOUR

JERO FLIPPED A veggie burger over on the grill, feeling Nayely's and Martha's eyes on him from across the beach. They were talking about him; he could always tell.

The sun was sinking lower, and the beach clean-up was well under way; scores of locals and the odd tourist had already filled a pile of rubbish bags with washed up flip-flops and plastic bottles. His eyes found Ivy, deeply involved as he'd guessed she might be if she showed up… which she had done, an hour late.

He'd spent that hour thinking maybe she wouldn't come.

They'd shared something intimate with those mantas. It had gone beyond all physical contact, or even words. Something had changed in that moment, being with her in the water. On the boat after that, the air had felt physically charged. He could have sworn she felt it too— the way she'd avoided his eyes but couldn't keep hers off his body. The secret thrill had made him ask her here, to something that wasn't work-related.

He was regretting it already. The more he found his eyes roving her figure as she followed the shoreline in a long sea-green sundress, the more he felt unsettled. She even looked good picking up rubbish.

He flipped another burger on the grill and served three hungry customers, irritated at the way he couldn't keep his eyes off her, bathed in the final streaks of sunlight. The woman was leaving in a matter of weeks, and even if he did go 'there' with tourists, which he absolutely did not, she was *working* with him. Around Aayla. The last thing he needed was for things to get complicated.

She was walking across the sand now, making a beeline for him. Damn, that long sundress was almost see-through in places, with the setting sun behind her. She was a knockout, in and out of the bikini he'd seen her in today.

'Hey, Ivy, you made it.'

She cast her amber eyes up and down his apron and tongs. 'Hey, yourself, chef.'

He was about to offer her his speciality—grilled shrimp and pineapple skewers—when Aayla bounded over, pigtails flying, covered in sand. He handed her a wet towel for her hands, which she ignored. 'Ivy! Did you bring your camera?'

'Not tonight…sorry,' she said, holding her empty hands up while Aayla pouted.

'Ivy's camera is not your toy,' he reminded her, handing her the towel again, and Aayla rolled her eyes, swiping at her dirty hands with it for all of three seconds before handing it to Ivy.

Ivy held the towel at arm's length, as if it were some strange, foreign artefact he'd just dug up from a Mayan tomb. He bit back a smile, tossing it into a rubbish bag for her.

'Ivy, I thought of a new game we can play with the puppies tomorrow,' Aayla said, eyes bright.

'Why don't you go play with Sasha?' he cut in, tossing a sausage in a bun for another customer.

She ignored him, casting her usual beseeching gaze up at Ivy. 'We can teach them to roll over!'

'Aayla…'

'I think they're a little young to roll over,' Ivy answered, passing him the ketchup when she saw he had his hands full. 'Maybe when they get adopted, their new parents can teach them that?'

Aayla frowned thoughtfully. Jero was about to direct her towards her playdate again, but Ivy had another idea. 'We could try teaching them to sit if you like? Most puppies pick that up pretty quickly if we give them treats.'

Aayla's eyes lit up. 'Can we photograph them, while they learn?'

'Maybe. Let me think about it.'

Aayla seemed to think that was an appropriate answer and skipped away up the beach happily. He felt a sigh of relief escape into his barbecue smoke.

For some reason, Aayla seemed drawn to Ivy, even without the camera. She had taken to shadowing Ivy in the clinic after school, and, OK, so they'd been feeding the puppies, and caring for Pluma together, which constituted more as work than hanging out, but still. Aayla got attached easily, no thanks to a lack of a mother figure in her life, and all of this…well, this had been his fear from the start: that his daughter would be crushed once someone else she admired sped off on the tourist boat and never returned.

'You know, I've been thinking,' Ivy said now, scraping a hand through her wild curls and making the orange rays reflect off the silver bracelet around her slender wrist. 'It was pretty impressive, how you got me to switch off down there today with the mantas. You took me out of my head and put me somewhere else. That doesn't happen a lot.'

'Is that so?'

She half smiled at the ocean, then him. 'I

didn't think about my emails for at least twenty minutes.'

He laughed and she shrugged. 'Sounds stupid, sure, but that's a big deal for me. I wanted to say thank you, Jero, for taking me in the way you have since we met. It means a lot.'

She turned to face him, and there it was again in her eyes: the look that spoke volumes of abject sadness, and secrets, and some kind of profound loss that had propelled her to escape into her work, even *before* she'd arrived at the Aqua Breeze Couples' Resort all alone. It made her infinitely more vulnerable to him, and he stopped himself conjuring another carnal fantasy about seeing her with that dress off.

He hadn't asked her any personal questions yet that could be construed as getting too close. Hmm. That *was* pretty selfish of him. Maybe she'd been waiting for him to ask and assumed that he just didn't care. The fact that she was here for work, to learn and to be of use was no restitution for his guilt suddenly.

'I'm happy I could help,' he told her truthfully. 'And you're helping *me* more than you know already. Your experience is invaluable.' He put down the tongs and untied his apron as his friend Nige slapped him on the back and offered to take over the barbecue duties.

'Let's go for a walk,' he said, checking Aayla

was still under the supervision of Sasha's mum, as was their agreement while he was on grill duty. 'I have something I think you should see.'

She cocked an eyebrow. 'Intriguing.' Then she hesitated on the spot, as if she wasn't sure if she should leave the scene either. Was he making her nervous after that 'moment' earlier today? 'I can't be long,' she said, eyeing the crowd around the shoreline. 'I do have to get back to work.'

'What work?'

'I run a clinic…'

'How could I forget?' he teased, and she fixed her eyes on him with such piercing effect he wished he hadn't said it. 'Are you going to sell up?' he asked her, remembering she'd mentioned some private equity company trying to buy them out.

Her face fell a second. 'I don't know yet. I don't know what else I'd do if I didn't work there. It's been my whole life.'

'Work isn't your *whole* life though, is it?'

'I love my work,' she clipped. Then she sighed and huffed a laugh. 'I know, I know… I should switch off more. Everyone tells me that.'

'I can always dunk you in the ocean again, if that will help,' he offered, and her mouth twitched again.

'I suppose a little walk won't hurt.'

They headed up the beach, and around the

rocks and he couldn't tell if he was unnerving her after earlier, or if she really was so into her work that she couldn't be away for more than an hour.

'I guess your partner must be freaking out without you, in Galway?' he asked as they took the narrow pathway that curved around the huge round boulders together, up, up, up towards the sky and what he knew would take her breath away.

'Mike is fine on his own,' she answered, lifting fistfuls of her sundress to walk easier. 'He always has everything under control.'

'So why are you working on your honeymoon? For your clinic as well as mine?'

The question lingered on the breeze for a moment as a flock of white butterflies fluttered from a shrub between the rocks, engulfing them in a moving cloud. Maybe he shouldn't have called it 'honeymoon', knowing she was alone.

'I guess work is just how I survive…when things fall apart,' she answered, before tripping on her dress and almost slipping off the path.

'Careful!' Deftly he caught her elbow, looping an arm around her waist till she was steady. Her breath came fast as her palms flattened hard against his chest. One second. Two seconds. She didn't move. He didn't let her go.

'What fell apart?' His lips were an inch from

her temple. More sunset butterflies swooped on the wind around them.

'We called the wedding off over half a year ago.' She gulped. 'I shouldn't have come here but... I didn't want to waste the booking. I'd also wanted to see this place my whole entire life. Now I know why.'

Jero's arm was still protecting her; maybe unnecessarily now. The ocean sparkled seductively beyond. Her curls were being lifted by the breeze and blown around his own head, trying to pull him under her perfumed spell.

Man, what is happening to you?

'Well, here you are,' he stated, releasing her, hoping she hadn't noticed his manhood rising to attention in his shorts, as it had today, being close enough to kiss her in her bikini.

'Here I am,' she replied, and the statement felt as loaded as a gun.

In minutes the chatter of the people on the beach was silenced by the ocean and the wind whipping up the grass along the ledge above the boulder wall. The pillar-box-red moss and liverwort carpets danced amid vivid purple flowers. This was one of his favourite meadows on Santa Cruz. It was even more magnificent in the sunset light.

The buteries had multiplied now, swooping in a synchronised show around the flowers as if to present each one to them. Beside him, Ivy reached for the camera that wasn't there and then grimaced regretfully.

Her dress flapped around both of their ankles as he watched her taking it in. 'It's so magical, Jero. The colours, the...'

'*Butterflies,*' he heard her continue under her breath as she shot a sideways glance his way. Amber eyes, flecked with yet more green and earthy browns in the sunset. The depths of them thrilled him and sent a shockwave of fear pulsing through his veins all at once.

'Come. This isn't even what I wanted to show you.'

He considered turning back, introducing Ivy to some more people, anything so they wouldn't be alone, where he'd think about kissing her again. He'd wanted to today in the water when the waves had pushed her close enough to jab him with her hipbones.

But here they *both* were. And he did want to show her Enrique.

He forced himself to carry on up the path ahead of her, right through the meadow. 'So, did your fiancé do something unforgivable?' he heard himself say. Well, how could someone like Ivy go from being engaged, to honeymooning on her own?

'Not really.'

She was quiet a moment, then she caught up to him on the path. The butterflies were parting for them as they walked, he realised now, as if they were royals in a crowd.

'I think it's better if we don't…you know… get into it,' she continued tightly.

Damn. Was that going a step too far? 'OK.'

As if sensing his disappointment, she pursed her lips and sighed through them. 'It's just that it's over, you know… Maybe it was over long before it was actually…over.'

'How long were you together?'

'Four years. We met in the park. I was taking pictures of the wild poppies and I noticed this tall guy, around my age. He was having trouble bending down to pick something up. Turned out his dog had made a mess…and Simon…that was his name…had done his back in, falling off his bike. He couldn't bend down far enough to pick it up. I offered to help him out.'

'You met because you helped him with a poo bag? Now that's romance.' Jero chuckled, and thankfully so did Ivy.

'It actually was, for a while. I took him food to his place while he couldn't bend down to his oven. When he was better, he took me out for dinners, I got to know Bernie, his Staffie. His mum liked me too. We had a nice time.'

He cocked an eyebrow at her. 'Just nice?'

'Nice was what I needed then,' she said tightly. 'It was grown up, you know, none of the mind games you get with online dating, and, believe me, I'd had plenty of that before I met him. It all took up far more time than it was worth, and I was busy, you know? I guess I was ready for someone, something serious, and easy. He told me he loved me after a month.' She looked at him sideways. 'Then, after four years he decided he wanted a family.'

'And you didn't?'

Ivy shrugged and looked in the other direction. He could tell she regretted telling him that already. Because he had Aayla?

'So...how is it, being a single dad all the way out here?' she deflected.

Jero realised he was dying to know more. Did she say she loved him back after a month? Did she fall for him as hard, or as quickly? By the way she was speaking, he didn't think so. The guy wanting a family had killed it...but as she'd said, before that, she'd been ready for something, and *something* had come along.

He knew people who'd settled for 'almost right' and 'easy' and that was their prerogative. Personally, he could never do that. He lived for the fire, the fights and the making up. But then, he'd had all that with Suranne...and that hadn't worked out either.

He frowned to himself, suddenly uneasy. Her question lingered in the air.

'It's not easy doing it alone but I have help,' he said eventually. 'We have a great community here, and Aayla's a great kid. She's a complex being, the most altruistic little creature I've ever met. She genuinely cares about every living being more than herself.'

'I've noticed.' Ivy smiled.

'A lot like you, actually,' he noted now.

Ivy looked nervously at her fingernails, then at the horizon. 'I don't know if we have that much in common…except maybe growing up without one of our parents. Where are we going exactly?'

Jero pointed to the curve in the path and kept them walking. 'You lost a parent?'

'My dad died when I was four. He went out to watch the rugby with some friends. It was raining, the car swerved, I don't really know exactly…' She trailed off while he fought for the right words.

'My mother worked hard to keep us both going. Even if it also meant I never saw her. I guess I was mostly parented by my dog, which might explain some things.'

She huffed a self-deprecating laugh and Jero drew a breath through his teeth. *Tough childhood indeed.* What could he say?

He led her on towards where he hoped Enrique would still be nesting, and asked if she had siblings, to which she replied no. No aunts or uncles either, so therefore no cousins. She'd had a nanny, she said, and books. Not many peers or friends. Maybe she'd thrown herself into work all these years to feel seen, and wanted?

Sounded kind of familiar. He'd done that too, albeit later in life.

The possibility of Suranne leaving him for someone else had never ever crossed his mind, until he'd come home that day and found her halfway out of the door. Their dates on her holiday here had been a lot of fun and, yes, the pregnancy had been a mistake, but he'd found himself excited by the prospect of fatherhood; excited to make things work with Suranne. He'd been infatuated with her; blind to the notion that he was just a holiday romance that had got way out of control.

The wedding had been fast, and far too soon, her pregnant belly stretching out her mother's old lace dress. He'd thought he'd been doing the right thing. She'd told him she wanted the same things. But she'd been young, eight years his junior. Looking back, maybe she'd just been scared of the alternative. In spite of becoming the mother to his child, she'd soon realised he wasn't her future.

After the birth, she'd suffocated under the weight of the new parental responsibilities, slipped away right in front of him; he'd just been too blind to see it.

He'd taken on a lot after she left. Maybe more than he knew how to handle. At first it had helped him not to dwell on the separation process, but all the nights he'd spent in the dark, battling a screaming hurricane of recurring nightmares in which Aayla disappeared on him, too...those had damn near squeezed his soul out irrevocably.

The whole drawn-out divorce had only hammered home that he'd been replaced by the mother of his child. He'd tried not to take it personally—a woman eight years younger than him was bound to want different things. Someone so headstrong and ambitious—all the traits he admired—was bound to change her mind a thousand times, but he was a proud man. He loathed feeling downgraded. Discarded, like the fishtails left by seagulls after the feast.

For a long time he'd hoped she'd come back, for Aayla's sake, of course. Not his. He could learn to live without her; in fact, he had. He'd risen from the ashes, toughened up and started over. A betrayal of that magnitude had left him no choice. But why should Aayla have to do the same? Why should *she* ever have to feel unwanted?

'What is that?' Ivy's eyes had grown wide, three metres from the huge grassy bundle of a nest, directly on the sandy floor. It was sheltered from the wind by some shrubs. An army of tiny lizards scurried away as they stepped closer. He touched a hand to the base of her spine, registering the way she flinched at the lizards, then inched closer to him all in one second.

'That's Enrique.'

They were less than a foot from the giant bird. The sun gleamed across her humongous yellow beak. 'She's an albatross. Majestic, isn't she? She's built this right here on the path because she trusts no one will step on it. It's like she knows she's protected by humans if we know where she is. It wouldn't happen anywhere else.'

Ivy looked enchanted. 'It wouldn't, you're right. Why did you call a female bird Enrique?'

'The rangers thought she was he, till they saw her with the eggs. She probably fights off iguanas every day, but she seems to like this spot.'

Jero watched Ivy circle the nest, hitching up her dress to her milky white ankles, keeping a respectful distance. She crouched to get a better look at the giant white bird. Its beady all-seeing eyes were scrutinising her just as hard. The light was fading fast now. They'd have to get back before Aayla missed him, but it felt pretty good to show Ivy things only the Galapagos Islands had to offer. Things he and Aayla loved to share.

Which was weird, and a little worrying…

'She's wonderful,' Ivy told him from the ground.

'She's going to be a great mother,' he replied, refocusing on the albatross and not on Ivy's lips. He crouched opposite her, the grassy, tangled stick nest between them. The giant bird shuffled and ruffled her feathers, clearly proud to be showcasing her future offspring still cocooned in their off-yellow eggshells.

'I guess *some* creatures are just meant to be mothers,' Ivy said wistfully, almost to herself. Her face seemed darker in a heartbeat. 'Some, on the other hand, are not.'

He frowned. 'What do you mean?'

'Does it have to mean anything?' she said, standing up.

Touché.

Wasn't that what he'd said about his tattoo earlier? That hadn't been entirely fair but why get into how the Mayan symbols in the manta ray translated as the lyrics of a song he'd written for Suranne? A waste of a good song, etched on his skin for ever. A reflection of the way he'd failed Aayla in every damn mirror.

'You're doing a really good job with Aayla,

if it means anything,' Ivy said, as if reading his mind, and he grunted his thanks. Maybe it looked as if he were, most of the time, on the outside. He'd failed her, not fighting harder to keep her mother around. Aayla had asked for her incessantly after Suranne left, but Suranne had asked him to keep away. He'd been torn, proud, hurt, but it would have been worse for his daughter if he'd given in to her pleas, if he'd gone to her and submitted Aayla to more rejection, wouldn't it?

He still didn't quite know how to feel; it nagged him, the thought that he should have done *something* more.

They retraced their route back to the beach in a somewhat awkward silence, pretending to be peaceful and tranquil, and he thought about what Ivy had said for the rest of the night.

So, he couldn't be sure, but, from what she'd said about her ex earlier, Ivy didn't want children of her own…or she'd decided motherhood was not for her. One of those assertions was correct, probably thanks to her own mother never being around when she was a kid. Children were scarred by stuff like that; he should know.

What with her broken engagement too, Ivy might have had her heart battered even harder than his over the years—and that was saying a lot.

He could show her how cool kids could be, though. There were all kinds of ways to see the world if you looked at it as children did. As Aayla did, his miracle daughter who had an age-defying understanding of the importance of these islands, and their inhabitants and struggles, even at six years old. Compassionate, empathetic, still awestruck by the beauty and wonders of the universe. His everything.

But you failed her, Jero. You failed to keep hold of her mother. The one thing she needs as much as you.

Tomorrow would be a fresh start, he decided as he tucked his daughter into bed that night. No more getting waylaid. No more falling under that Irish spell. However Ivy did it, he was now rendering himself impervious to her charms. Only a fool would let his heart and mind get tangled up like a dolphin in a fishing net over a tourist with one foot out of the door and more emotional baggage than him.

He'd be polite and present, but he would not get any more personal with Ivy Malone. And he definitely wouldn't let Aayla get too close either.

CHAPTER FIVE

'WHERE IS IT?'

'Where is what?' Ivy had to bite her tongue watching Jero and Dudders, the dreadlocked hemp-dressed volunteer from Birmingham by way of Thailand, both rifling through cardboard boxes full of Manila files in the storeroom, which doubled as a caging area. 'The adoption agency paperwork. I swear I put it here. We need the details for a litter we sent over to Quito.'

'Isn't it in the system?' she asked, turning her attention back to little Pluma, who was fluffing up her wings, probably looking out for Aayla.

Aayla was due in from school any minute. The bird had taken to following her around the place whenever she was here, a lot like Aayla followed *Ivy*.

'The files *are* the system,' Dudders reminded her in his thick midlands accent. 'But I wrote the details down myself. I think.'

Dudders' brows met thoughtfully. His loose

elephant-patterned pants billowed in the AC as he stood, racking his brains. A tiny growl, not unlike a sea lion's, rumbled at the back of Jero's throat. 'You *think*?'

Ivy scooped up Pluma and held her close to her chest. 'I can help you organise things a little better if you like?' she offered. Then she waited, expecting the usual brush-off.

'It's fine, we're handling it,' Jero huffed as predicted. She bit her tongue, stroking Pluma's soft brown head with gentle fingers, feeling the tame bird nestle its sky-blue webbed feet further into one hand. So Jero really didn't want her help. Fine.

Not fine at all!

He'd been a little stand-offish for the last couple of days. Once or twice, he'd gone out on call without her and taken Aayla for the 'experience'. She'd been left to handle consultations, and had even performed a couple of small surgeries, always with injectable anaesthetic to keep costs down. Always with one of the volunteers close at hand.

Their vet nurse was a twenty-five-year-old guy from Guayaquil called Zenon, with tattoos of flowers all the way up his left arm and right leg. He was an insult to symmetry but wore a smile that could melt butter, when he showed up on time. Which was less often than she'd have liked.

Dudders was reliable enough, after a little gentle encouragement. She suspected at times that he'd done little at the monkey sanctuary in Thailand besides slip his favourites bananas and play them Bob Marley from his hammock. He'd certainly told her 'that was the best part about it, mate,' a few too many times for it to be a joke, but he was here, and who was she to judge?

All in all, it was the rewarding experience she'd hoped for. Not relaxing at all but humbling indeed. And a stark contrast from everything she was used to back home.

It was still amazing to her that veterinary care at the Darwin Animal Clinic was all provided free of charge. They didn't put a price on saving lives as they did—unfortunately—in her part of the world. Families could bring in their animals for free parasite treatments, which helped protect the fragile Galapagos ecosystem. It was all about giving back, ensuring all animals and people lived in harmony.

But she would rather be contributing *with* Jero when it came to protecting the birthplace of evolutional theory, out there in the field. Not in here all the time. Or…she'd be fine in here actually if he were here, too.

Either way.

Oh, Lord. She was doomed.

Maybe he'd still invite her on the expedition with him later, she thought, training her eyes on his handsome profile in the sunlight. It was an overnight voyage with a conservationist this time, to check on the endemic waved albatross, known for their wingspan of up to two and a half metres. Unlike Enrique, these birds preferred a more remote location on the far south-eastern tip of the Galapagos archipelago. Some twenty thousand pairs were thought to breed and nest on Española Island—an island that was almost four million years old and totally uninhabited.

Hmm. Ivy watched the muscles turn to rocks in Jero's arms as he pulled more files from the shelf. The mysterious manta almost smirked at her from his arm. There was more to all that cryptic lettering than he was letting on. The design was too intricate, the symbolism too carefully considered to be meaningless.

Again. Why did she care?

For the same reason she wanted to go to a tiny four-million-year-old island covered in albatross poop with him, she supposed. But getting closer wouldn't do her any good. The more she cared, the harder it would be to forget him—them—when she had to.

Already Aayla was a little ray of sunshine, who brightened every room they shared. It had kind of sneaked up on her, the burst of surprise joy at hearing her unique, fresh, often hilarious take on things. Hmm. She'd never thought of her life as being anything but childfree, but Simon's words kept coming to her unannounced now:

'You just think you'd be a bad mother because your own mother was. Abandonment is not a hereditary disease, you know, it's a choice. If you chose motherhood, you'd throw your all into it, like you do everything else.'

Of course, she'd always poo-pooed him, told him it wasn't anything to do with abandonment, that she was just too busy to choose that, and too set in her ways. All of which was true, but maybe he knew her better than she thought he did.

Nuzzling Pluma's head to her chin, she watched Jero sink into the worn leather desk chair and swing his big feet up onto the desk. She liked his leather sandals, they were nomadic and comfortable and a little worn, like Jero.

Suddenly, Simon was gone from her head.

God, that moment with the mantas the other day, that had been *real*.

And the other moment, when she'd stumbled on the path up to the meadow and he'd caught her, eyes full of sunset and surrounded by butterflies. A movie moment! But *real*. The kind of real that stole your breath and threatened to lift you clean off the floor, and proved to you that any other encounter before it was only sub-par. It had taken all her strength not to surrender to her impulses and kiss his impossibly perfect mouth…

'Found it!' Jero pulled a file from a box and held it up triumphantly. Ivy forced a smile. How they could live with such organised chaos was still beyond her.

'Ivy! Papa! Did the puppies sit good when you told them to?'

Aayla all but launched herself into the room. Her nanny, a petite Ecuadorian twenty-some-thing called Nina with hair down to her back-side, was close on her heels.

'Not yet, I think they're waiting to sit when *you* tell them to,' Ivy said, surprising herself. That had come out of her effortlessly, without thinking. It was the truth, after all. Aayla seemed to have a real gift with the animals.

Aayla whispered to them as Ivy used to whisper to Zeus. She also sat with them for hours in silence, as she'd done with Zeus. She could have sworn that dog's big old heart used to understand every single word she did or didn't say.

Dropping her school bag to the floor, Aayla, in jean shorts and a shirt covered in tiny clouds and rainbows, got to her knees by the box of puppies. Ivy's heart skidded seeing Jero forget about his annoyance over the filing system, or lack thereof, instantly. He got down to her level in his scrubs and asked about her day. So sweet. And sexy, and…extraordinarily patient.

Aayla was getting assigned a pen pal, someone in her grade, but from a different country. Aayla had a papaya smoothie for lunch *and* her class picked the fruits for it. Aayla got top marks in 3D biology, whatever that was to a six-year-old. Aayla wanted to braid Ivy's hair.

'Wait, what?' Ivy sprang from where she'd perched on the desk with Pluma, away from Aayla's little hands. Dudders pulled on a white coat over his elephant pants and made a swift exit out to the reception area to greet the young couple walking in.

'I know how to braid hair. I can practise on you. I like your hair, Ivy.'

How do I get out of this?

Like a gladiator on a rearing war horse, Jero made a human blockade of himself and coaxed Aayla quickly out of the storeroom after Dudders, where she was fortunately distracted by the family's cat in a cage, and Nina the nanny.

Crisis avoided.

'I'll try and keep her out of your way,' Jero said, turning back to her. His stance was uncomfortable in the doorway. Suddenly she wanted anything but.

'No, no, she's fine,' she assured him, crouching to open Pluma's cage, feeling his eyes on her back. 'It's just the curls, you know. It wouldn't braid all that well. She'd only be disappointed.'

Jero made a huffing sound, re-stuck a peeling poster to the wall behind the cages and pulled another file out for the family in Reception.

Ugh.

Ugh to that no doubt illegible and useless file in his sexy big man hands, and ugh to the excuse. Jero wasn't blind, she'd just given him further proof of how incompetent she was when it came to stuff like that…physical contact, motherly kind of stuff.

Her friends used to laugh at her, refusing to hold their babies. Only now she was realising why she'd refused. It always felt too risky. What if she liked it? What if she wanted one? What if one arrived, and she was nothing but a disappointment?

That accidentally spoken out loud statement, when she'd told Jero how only *some* creatures were meant to be mothers—he'd probably thought she'd been dissing Suranne, his ex-wife, as if it were *her* business to be making observations like that.

Aayla's mother wasn't exactly beating down doors to see her, sure, but at least the girl had a father. A bloody good one at that.

'Look, Jero…'

She was about to explain herself and tell him how sorry she was that kids had somehow fallen into the 'strange little aliens that unnerve me' category in her mind. But she was halted by Pluma, who was all but wrestling from her hands.

To her shock, the dozy little bird dived a foot from her crouched stance, waddled right through Jero's legs, and out of the door towards Aayla. Aayla scooped her up lovingly in her arms and kept her away from the puppies, talking to them all as a group like a shepherdess comforting her flock.

'What the…?'

'Ivy, look, she loves me, and I love her.' Aayla's voice was gentle and soft, but she looked elated. Her happiness was infectious. The urge to explain herself shot straight from Ivy's mind.

'A baby blue-footed booby thinks a six-year-old girl is her mother.' Jero scraped a hand across his head. The sleeve of his scrubs rubbed up to hers as she joined him in the doorway. Hopefully her smile hid the way her impossible heart was revving like a race car at the contact.

'She's never going to get rid of that bird now. They've bonded,' he said, so only she could hear. She forced her eyes to stay on Aayla. His warm breath tickled her ear, rearranging her senses.

She was back on that boulder-lined path in her head, pressed against him, nerve-endings fraying all over again.

'We should make sure that doesn't happen, really.'

She swallowed. *We.* Which unfortunate bonding were they talking about exactly?

'They're wild,' he reminded her. 'We don't keep them here. You can't keep anything with wings anywhere it doesn't want to be.'

'What do you think cages are for?' she retorted, flustered.

Jero huffed a laugh. 'Nothing needs a cage if it likes where it is,' he said. 'But the thing about wild creatures is, you never know when they're going to change their mind.'

Ivy kept her mouth shut, even as his eyes on her cheek made her hot. Did he mean her?

It could never be a fling with Jero, she realised like a slap to her cheeks. Even if her mounting crush had twisted her daydreams into passionate kisses with him on windy outcrops. Wasn't his ex a tourist, who'd left them both for another life? What was the likelihood he'd go there again, even if he wanted to? *How about...zero to none?*

'So, that conservationist—her name is Dee Whitfield. She wants to know if you're coming with us on the overnighter,' he said now, looking at her sideways. 'She read about your credentials; I think she's keen for you to join us.'

Oh, so now you're bringing it up.

Ivy felt hot under her collar now. How nice that her excellent professional reputation preceded her. That was not entirely surprising, if she did say so herself. But it was definitely best not to tempt disaster on *her* side, with Jero. Remote sailing, open waters, rugged island terrain, Jero's gym-honed body with his shirt off in the sun, administering animal care, maybe some more snorkelling with exotic wildlife…it would be torture.

'I should probably stay here,' she forced herself to say. 'You've been doing a lot of these trips without me anyway.'

Jero's mouth twisted, then he shrugged at the floor. The opportunity hovered between them like a leaden ball on a ceiling chain, and the next five seconds in her mind went something like: *I'll go. I won't go. Oh, why not, I'll go. What? No, I absolutely won't go.*

This is ridiculous. Visiting one of the planet's most isolated archipelagos is an amazing opportunity. Besides, the conservationist will be there. What could you possibly get up to in such close quarters?

'OK, if the conservationist wants to meet me, how can I refuse? Consider me on the voyage,

Captain,' she said, before she could think any more about it.

'I won't be steering the yacht tonight,' Jero replied.

Her mouth fell open. A yacht?

He offered her an infuriating smile that only made his mouth look all the more kissable. 'I'm just kidding—we save those for the tourists. I'll bring the seasickness pills. Don't forget your waterproof jacket. Oh, do you have a zoom lens for your camera?'

'Of course, why?'

'It's the best place for bird-watching in the Galapagos. Aayla loves telling the cruise shippers what's what.'

'Aayla's coming?' Ivy swallowed an albatross-egg-sized knot from her throat as Jero glanced at his daughter, then back at her. He looked mildly irritated by something now.

'I just remembered, Nina's off this weekend. She'll *have* to come with us.'

Ivy forced an upbeat tone that still somehow came out kind of choked. 'Well, this will be fun.'

CHAPTER SIX

'ARE YOU ASLEEP YET?' Jero was standing outside her cabin door. Her breathing caught like a
kite on a washing line as she pictured him there,
one hand poised to knock if she didn't answer.

He'd already asked her if she wanted a nightcap and, while she'd wanted nothing more after
such a long, exhausting day in the heat, she'd
felt the chemistry bubbling up between them
the second Dee, their resident conservationist, a
sixty-something-year-old Brit from the Galapagos Conservation Trust, and Aayla had gone to
bed. She'd refused the nightcap, but now, just as
predicted, she was lying awake, trying and fail-
ing to allow the gently rhythmic bobbing of the
ocean below them to lull her into sleep. Thinking about him.

'I'm awake,' she answered, somewhat against
her will.

'Then you shouldn't miss this!' he replied. 'I'm
guessing you don't have this back in Galway.'

Intrigue won her over.

Out on the deck, Jero ushered her behind a long, protruding telescope he'd focused on the stars. No sooner had she pressed one eye to the rounded end than a barrage of shooting stars lit up the sky, right in front of her.

'Woah!' She staggered backwards in awe, right into him, and he laughed as his hands landed on her shoulders, then fell to her hips. Her pulse became a meteor in her veins on the spot. Jero guided her eyes back to the telescope, then wheeled it into a new position before placing his hands right back where they'd just been, over her hips. She could literally feel the heat of him against her back, making her burn. Did he have any idea what he was doing to her?

'Did you know, you can see twice as many stars in the Galapagos as anywhere else?' he whispered softly as she scanned the sparkly skies.

She swallowed and shook her head. Words wouldn't find her; everything was blowing her mind in this moment.

'It's because we're on the equator,' he continued. 'It means the constellations from both hemispheres meet in the middle. On nights like this, it looks like the heavens are literally exploding.'

Ivy caught her breath. After a long moment

of silence, during which she willed her heart to stop skidding around like a bumper car, she said, 'I wonder if my dad's up there somewhere, orchestrating this show for us somehow. He was kind of a star when I was a kid. To me, anyway.'

'I bet you were a pretty awesome kid, Ivy,' he said.

She dared to turn around. Jero was looking at her, really looking at her, as if he wanted to say something else but was holding it back. They studied each other's eyes for what felt like far too long before he looked away. Then he said, 'I don't know if I believe in an afterlife, do you?'

She shrugged, stepping back from the telescope. He'd snatched back the magic somehow, as if their closeness had freaked him out, too.

Dragging a hand through her hair, she watched him reposition the telescope and press his own eye to the end. 'I should go, try and get some sleep,' she told his back, and scuttled off to her cabin before he could respond. She slept fitfully till the seagulls woke her up at dawn.

Isla Española was, without a shadow of a doubt, the most beautiful place Ivy had ever set eyes on. The dramatic setting was even more perfect than the prettiest parts of Santa Cruz. Her camera just couldn't do justice to the towering black lava cliffs, the never-ending rhythmic crashing and rolling of the waves below, and the gamut of colourful seabirds swooping around them fearlessly on the wind.

Aayla did indeed know each and every one of them.

'Look, Daddy! Another cactus finch,' she cried out now, waving the binoculars at Jero from her place ahead of them on the grassy trail. Little Pluma, who'd come along for the ride, poked her white fluffy head out from the tiny Disney backpack that was slung over the girl's shoulders. Ivy still couldn't believe she'd brought the bird, but Jero was right, they'd bonded and Pluma wouldn't have fared well, being left alone. She only ate worms from their hands now.

They were forty minutes into their walk in the area of Punta Suarez, heading towards a well-known albatross nesting ground. So far, Aayla had blown Ivy's mind with her knowledge of the island's habitat. Even Dee was suitably impressed, which was saying something, because Dee seemed to know everything about everything. Though maybe not as much as Jero and Aayla.

'Oh, look, there's a Galapagos hawk coming in. Ivy, you have to take a photo!'

Aayla was intent on capturing everything with the camera. Ivy caught Jero's smile as he shook something off the heel of his hiking boot that looked suspiciously like a clump of lizard poop. He caught her hand as she stepped back to avoid landing in any other insalubrious debris, and narrowly missed crushing a bird's egg that was nestled in a shrub.

Adrenaline flooded her veins at his touch. 'Careful there.'

'Thanks.' She fell deep into his eyes again as he lifted his sunglasses momentarily. His loose white shirt flapped open in the breeze, framing his broad chest and the faded Texas Longhorns football shirt he'd pulled on this morning, after their swim off the boat.

It hadn't been easy, keeping her eyes off him, or keeping away from him in the water. But she'd managed to swim on her back, metres away, grateful that Aayla and Dee had been there as a buffer. It all felt a bit too close for comfort, especially after last night.

On any other guy, that football shirt might have made her cringe. So would the baseball hat, she mused now, observing flecks the colour of Ireland's autumn leaves in the browns of his eyes. Jero wasn't exactly your typical football fan. He knew every shrub and flower, and every bird's call that came at them on this path. He knew about the various marine and air currents that saw different creatures settling on different islands, and when he spoke, she listened, absorbing it all in wonder, like a child.

She'd never been anywhere as wild. It wasn't all butterflies, birds and perfection, but to witness him and Aayla out here enjoying this purity together tugged at something deep in her chest, a kind of untethering and unravelling. She couldn't quite put her finger on the feeling.

'Be careful with it, but I think you should take the photo,' she told Aayla, catching up with her on the path and switching out her binoculars for the camera.

'Are you sure?' Jero whispered in her ear.

'Why not? The kid is clearly excited to learn photography,' she replied, securing the camera around Aayla's neck by the strap.

A delighted Aayla snapped away at the birds in the trees and Ivy pressed her eyes to the tiny lenses of the binoculars, focusing in on the rare hawk. Hopefully the gadget would hide her flushed cheeks—why did her heart turn into a raging bull every time Jero so much as brushed her ear with his breath?

'What do we have over here?' She looked up just as Jero put a hand on one shoulder and gently prised the binoculars from her with the other. 'Can I see for a second?'

Suddenly Dee was squealing in excitement, squinting into her own binoculars up ahead of them. Aayla started twisting the telephoto lens of her camera in a way that did make her unsure about the loan, actually…but Jero thrust the binoculars back at her, redirecting her attention.

'What are we looking at?' she asked him.

'Just the elaborate courtship rituals of the mighty albatross,' he said through his wide grin. 'These birds mate for life. It's quite something to see this for yourself, look!'

The warmth of his hands clasped over hers made her brain turn to mush. Then her eyes found what he was showing her. She couldn't help the smile stretching out her face, especially as all three of them started laughing and commenting on what they were looking at, as if they'd been thrown into a studio to record a soundtrack on behalf of David Attenborough.

Two giant albatrosses were dancing seductively on the rocks ahead, stopping every now and then to clap and smack their beaks together like swords.

'See how the female tilts her head back and cries out like that?' Jero's mouth tickled her ear again, making her shiver. 'That's albatross code for, I quite like you. I might want to have your babies.'

Ivy grinned and turned her head, almost knocking him on the nose with the binoculars. Swiftly he pulled them from her hands, and she froze to find him less than an inch from her face. 'Sorry,' she said too quickly.

'You're a hazard,' he teased. His narrowed eyes grazed her lips, and she could have sworn, for just a fraction of a second, she literally *saw* him think about kissing her.

Then he turned to Aayla, swiping a hand across his mouth and jaw as if he were physically squishing the thought. Her heart began a steady thrum that was almost too loud. Head high, she smoothed down her shirt and shorts and carried on up the path towards Dee, cursing herself, avoiding his eyes.

That was close, dammit, too close for comfort. *But he definitely felt it too.*

So, her unfortunate crush might not all be one-sided. She couldn't help mulling it over as they all went about counting the albatrosses they came across in a considerate silence for the next two hours. Dee and Jero tagged the ones who weren't yet being monitored, and occasionally time stopped as a frolicking sea lion stole her attention from the task at hand.

She still couldn't quite look Jero in the eye, and he seemed to be steering himself and Aayla away from her at every opportunity.

The sooner they got back to Santa Cruz, the better, she told herself later, watching Jero push the chairs around the table ready for dinner on the deck of their boat. She pretended to be concentrating on some notes she'd taken earlier, but she couldn't stop looking at him from her lounge chair, wondering what he was thinking about earlier.

If he was thinking anything at all, she reminded herself. Men didn't romanticise every little encounter as women had the tendency to do. If only she could stop picturing him with his shirt off.

Never mind, I'll soon be back at the hotel, she told herself. She'd be back in control of her wandering thoughts, there.

'Almost time for dinner, Ivy, are you hungry?' Dee asked her from across the deck. She was setting the forks on the small table.

The sun was setting on their first day on Isla Española, and Aayla was busy photographing the last rays creeping over the wooden boat and the deep ocean they were bobbing on, offshore. *Nowhere to go now. No distractions.* Not even an Internet connection to aid the checking of her emails.

They ate their pasta and salad as the sun sank, and the captain of their trusty vessel, Manny, turned a series of lights on, sending shadows dancing across the deck. The ocean was quickly fading into black. It felt as if they were deep in space, with not another human or boat around for miles.

Aayla started yawning in her seat. Then she ran to her room and returned with *The Hungry Caterpillar*. 'Pluma wants you to read to her, Ivy,' she stated, crossing to the bird's small cage and letting her out to waddle freely around the hardwood floor. Her blue feet left little smacking sounds in her wake, but Ivy shifted in her chair at the familiar blast of discomfort.

Jero seemed to notice. He stood from his chair opposite hers, while Dee looked between them in interest, sipping on the last of her soup. 'Ivy doesn't want to read to anyone tonight. It's been a long day,' he told her firmly, taking the book from his daughter's hands. But Pluma was waddling straight towards her now and, in seconds, she'd hopped onto Ivy's lap, pinning her in her place.

'I swear, she understands what you say, Aayla.' Ivy laughed, struck with wonder as the bird burrowed into her lap on top of her napkin.

'I told you, she wants you to read to her.' Aayla took the book back from Jero and pushed it towards Ivy on the table. Pluma ruffled her feathers encouragingly and Jero let out a sigh, clearing their dishes and cutlery away as Dee excused herself and went to her cabin for the night.

'Maybe I should read to you, Aayla?' Ivy

heard herself offer. Jero looked unconvinced for a second, but she picked up the book and Aayla settled herself down for the story anyway. Ivy read half from memory, and half from badly translated Spanish under several more shooting stars. Jero's eyes burned into her from across the table. She stumbled over her words several times.

There was something unnerving that came with being around just the two of them, she realised. Their little family unit was something quite special, something sacred. Something she'd never had. It was cosy and warm, like pulling on a jumper fresh from the dryer. It made her feel snug and complete… right until she remembered she had absolutely no part in it. Not really. She *was* an outsider here. This thing would carry on without her, long after she was gone, picking up her life alone back in freezing-cold Galway. The clinic was all she had. Maybe she shouldn't sell, she thought suddenly, even if Mike told her he wanted to.

The thought of being without it suddenly made her feel quite vulnerable, like a baby bird left out in the open for the lizards. Her work was literally *all* she had.

The chemistry with Jero was still burning brighter than the stars by the time he left the deck to carry Aayla to her room. Ivy turned to the moon in its Milky Way hammock, listening to the little girl's sleepy giggles through the wall, watching the ripples across the ink-black water, anticipating his return.

Jero was behind her again in minutes, holding up a bottle of whisky and two glasses. 'How about a nightcap?'

He motioned to two lounge chairs side by side and every inch of her knew she should probably say no again and go to bed, as she'd been planning to since they'd finished dinner.

'OK. Why not?' she heard herself say anyway. *Curses.* She was doing what she'd avoided doing *last* night—immersing too much of herself in his all-too-captivating company—but it wasn't as if she could change her mind. He was already pouring her a drink. She didn't want to be rude.

Silence settled around them as she moved to the other lounge chair, taking Pluma with her. As if sensing the tension in the air, Jero started talking about their day, the albatrosses, the sea lions they'd be tagging tomorrow. He told her about a penguin who'd once sneaked on a boat like this behind him, and how he'd had to sail all the way back with it so as not to cross-contaminate the islands.

It could have been the whisky, but she started to relax.

Until he said, 'So, you told me you didn't want to get into it, and forgive me for asking, but I can't stop wondering how come your ex could have ever let you go.'

Her breath hitched in her throat.

'I mean, I don't know you very well.' Jero reached for the bottle again and, stunned, she held out her glass for one more. 'But I can tell you're smart, you're accomplished, you're beautiful, and you can make up a mean ending to *The Hungry Caterpillar*. Who knew he ended up adopting a blue-footed booby in the English version, like Aayla?'

Ivy rubbed her arms, trying to ignore the way him calling her beautiful felt like hot liquid honey filling the cracks in her heart. 'I told you, Simon wanted to start a family,' she admitted, taking herself by surprise.

Jero nodded, tapping his glass to the arm of the chair. 'And you weren't ready?'

'I don't think I'll ever be ready. I work too hard for all that.'

His eyes narrowed at her words. 'It's not easy,' he said quietly after a moment. 'Raising a kid. It's not something I ever anticipated doing alone, either.'

He swigged from his drink and stood up. Ivy

followed him, resting her arms on the railing and noting the moonlight in the water throwing ethereal, shimmering streaks on his skin. 'Why did your ex leave *you*?' she dared. 'You're smart, you're accomplished, you're beautiful.'

He grinned and nudged his shoulder to hers, swirling the ice in his glass until his mouth was a thin line again. 'I guess she wanted more than this island. After she left, I used to wake up in a sweat thinking Aayla was gone too. I used to race to her room at three a.m. just to check she hadn't sneaked away. Between you and me, sometimes I still do. She'll leave me one day, though. She'll want more than this island, too.'

He stole a sideways glance at her. She read his look like a book. He was terrified Aayla would leave him as his ex had. 'I don't think you need to worry about that just yet,' she said, softly, daring to place a hand over his. 'You're a great dad. Aayla seems happy, well adjusted...'

He studied her hand as if it were a rare, untrustworthy alien that had landed on him from the rings of Jupiter. 'I do my best.'

'She's wonderful. I, for one, enjoy her company. Really, that's the truth. Trust me, that is quite surprising. Coming from me...'

A storm blew over his features suddenly. He pulled his hand away and put his glass down on the deck, eyes like narrowed slits. 'So, when is your flight out of here again?'

What?

She watched him curl and flex his fingers, as if he was still shaking her touch away. He'd just let a wall down, then built it back up higher than ever. 'I… I don't know. I forget what day it is,' she said truthfully.

'Well, you'd better write it down. You don't want to get stuck here.'

'I guess not,' she replied coolly, even as her heart went berserk in her chest. She scanned his profile in the darkness. He was slipping away faster than he'd started to open up.

What had just happened? Oh, God, had she accidentally just insulted Aayla?

'What the hell?' Ivy jumped as, without warning, Jero gripped the railings, his knuckles white. She followed his eyes out to sea. A bright white light she hadn't seen before was flashing on and off in the distance. Even she knew it was far too close to Isla Española than what was allowed after dark. 'I don't believe it. They came back!' he spat, incredulous.

'Who came back?' Her heart was still skipping beats.

Jero darted for the cabin in his bare feet. She followed him in confusion, with Puma waddling after her. Manny was snoozing on a couch, but he sat bolt upright when Jero snatched up the radio and promptly called the coastguard.

CHAPTER SEVEN

'LAST TIME THEY CAME, they filled the hull with thousands of sharks and tuna. Tonnes of it.' Jero kept his eye on the vessel ahead, feeling his temperature rise with every second they drew closer. 'They wreaked havoc on land, too.'

Manny was doing his best to speed them towards the illegal trawler, but it was speeding away from *them* just as quickly. His head was a storm of possible outcomes. 'I probably don't need to tell you, Ivy, that wildlife trafficking is the third most profitable illegal activity after drug and weapon smuggling?'

'I did know that.' Ivy scrubbed her wild red hair from her forehead and held it back with one hand against the wind. 'I appreciate the education, Jero, but what exactly are you planning to do?'

He bit on his cheeks. Good question. Dee was watching Aayla and Pluma, safe inside, but who knew who was onboard that boat? Or what?

'You're not going to try and get on that boat, are you?' Ivy said now. She looked even paler than usual in the moonlight. How the hell was he supposed to answer her? There wasn't exactly a plan.

'All I know is the coastguard won't get here as fast as we need him to—the very reason these illegal traders try their luck out here is because we can't man every island around the clock, especially Española. It's too far away from everything else. Hey!' He yelled out over the roaring engine as the vessel came into full view. Ivy let go of her hair, mouth agape.

Her eyes grew wide and fearful all of a sudden. 'Jero…'

'Hey! Do you have a licence to be here?' he called out as Manny steered them close enough to see the guy on the deck, looking up at them. Of course, no one answered him. Crates and boxes of ice were sloshing water over the ship's deck, and he felt the chill of it run through his veins. They were planning to ice whatever they'd been trawling, which could be tonnes of fish and marine life, as before.

Manny swerved the boat again and it lunged as they caught a wave. Jero's heart stopped as Ivy slipped and almost skidded under the railings into the water. The ability to anticipate her next move overpowered him, as if it were coming from somewhere outside himself. He caught her, wrapped his arms about her waist and pulled her backwards against his chest, gripping the railing tight with his other hand before he could suffer the same fate.

'Don't make me dive in there after you!'

A stocky guy on the deck caught his eye. There were three of them now, leaning over the side, making wide, frenzied gestures at each other. He knew instinctively they were discussing when to pull up the nets.

'They know we would have called the coastguard. Whatever they've been trawling up to here will be destroyed if they pull up now,' he told Ivy over the wind.

Ivy pulled away from him. 'I need to get the camera! We need proof of what they're doing!'

'We need to stop them,' he replied, but she was already scrambling for her SLR. As Ivy snapped away, one hand on the railing so as not to fall again, the men scattered, obviously alarmed she might identify them.

'Nice!' Jero reached for the rope and anchor. Deftly he looped it around his arm and attempted to hook the ship.

'What if they've gone for weapons?' Ivy cried. The camera fell to her waist on its strap.

'We can't think that.' He urged her backwards gently out of potential harm's way and flung the lid off a box of tools. A knife—perfect. Another knife, this one longer and sturdier—even better.

Ivy shook her head as he slid them both into his pockets and attempted the hook again. This time it caught, just below the bow.

'What are you doing?' Her hands snatched the back of his shirt as he approached the railings and studied the shrinking gap between their boat and the bobbing trawler.

'I'm going to cut their nets. I just have to jump onto their lifeboat, see? I can reach them from there.'

Her fingers gripped his wrist. 'Are you crazy? What are you, James Bond of the Galapagos?'

He ignored her. 'It'll be carnage if they bring those nets up. If Aayla sees that…'

Manny was swerving close enough now that he could almost jump onboard. Manny would know what he was intending to do, he thought. They'd been over scenarios like this a thousand times—you did whatever you could to protect this place. The ocean was family, a provider and a friend. He'd taught Aayla that too, years ago. He put one foot up on the railing, ready to jump. To his horror, Ivy was beside him in a second.

'I'm coming with you,' she said now, climbing over the railings completely until she was leaning precariously over the open water, her skirt and hair a billowing flag.

'Get down, Ivy, they'll see you…'

Before he could stop her, she was leaping from the side and landing cat-like on all fours on the yellow-striped lifeboat. His stared at her in disbelief. *What the…?*

'Hurry up, then,' she snapped up at him. There was still no sign of the men on deck, though he could see one head bobbing up behind a window. They'd brave the deck again soon. It was now or never.

The floodlights from their boat just missed him as he took the leap over the thrashing water and landed with a thud beside her. Ivy bit back a smile as their eyes met, then both of them stumbled on the next wave, colliding and righting themselves together. Mutual admiration filled a millisecond window before he handed her a knife and they both got sawing.

They only had to loosen one side to throw it off kilter and ensure whatever these guys had captured would be thrown back into the water, instead of hoisted up onto the trawler. They had to work fast, but Ivy was as determined as him, working the knife with deft cutting movements and focus, even as the ocean spray soaked them to the bone.

'Hey!' A voice, from the deck. One of the men. 'What do you think you're doing?'

A bearded weathered face was peering down at them now, thrashing his arms about.

'They've seen us,' he told her. Ivy didn't stop her sawing. In fact she sped up.

'We're almost there, don't stop!' she urged.

'Daddy?' The voice from behind him, on their boat, was an ice-cold nitro blast to his bloodstream. *Aayla.*

'Daddy! Come back!' Aayla was awake and watching the scene in terror.

'Don't stop,' Ivy yelled again, but the guy who'd seen them was attempting to climb over the side of the trawler now, his yellow jacket a warning beacon. Would he drop to the lifeboat, to stop them himself, with a weapon, all while Jero's daughter looked on?

Suddenly, the net shifted. Ivy jumped backwards, almost tumbling to the floor again as it crashed towards them and swung out again, threatening to take them out with it. Jero caught her just as the tangle of fishing nets folded and collapsed with a heavy groan. Just a second ago it had looked as if it weighed a tonne, but now it was flapping emptily over their heads, blocking the guy's descent. Unfortunately, it also blocked their exit.

Ivy clutched his shirt at the collar, burying her head in his shoulder. He wrapped himself around her, and tried not to picture Aayla up there, watching all this. Her little mind must be spinning in fear.

Just then, a barrage of lights appeared on the horizon like soldiers. Beyond the nets, the sky lit up and whirring sounded above them. *Thank God.*

The helicopters almost drowned out his next words to Ivy. He breathed a sigh of relief into her hair, still cradling her head against him. The Galapagos National Park control centre must have monitored their trajectory and vectored a patrol vessel for an interdiction. Galapagos Park Rangers and Ecuadorian Navy officials would rescue them and see to it that these guys were locked away like the incorrigible scum they were.

Remarkably an emotional yet exhausted Aayla slept through all that followed their dramatic rescue and deposit back on their own boat. The night patrol, the buzz of radios, the clicking of cameras and the onslaught of questions made a wreck of his head. It was several hours before he and Ivy were alone, and their deck was quiet again, but he couldn't sleep.

Neither could Ivy apparently.

She found him on the deck, a blanket wrapped around her shoulders. She was clenching and un-clenching her fists with shock and nerves, and he poured her a warm tea from a flask, urged her to sit back down in the lounge chair.

'That wasn't exactly how I planned this night to go,' he told her wryly, and she hugged an arm around herself, eyeing him over her teacup.

'I just hope Aayla didn't get any ideas, watching us chase after criminals,' she said with a sardonic smile. He exhaled deeply and dropped to the other chair.

'So do I. Luckily she seemed to understand we had no choice.'

Ivy held his eyes. Then she put her cup down and took his hand across the gap, sending a warm cascade of comfort over his heart that almost made him recoil from her. 'You were amazing, thinking so quickly about what to do.'

'You jumped over there first,' he reminded her. For some reason, he was remembering the feel of his hand in her wet red hair on the lifeboat, how much he'd wanted to keep her safe, and keep her close.

She screwed up her face, wrinkled her nose, embarrassed maybe? 'I did, didn't I?' she said.

Whatever it was about her that kept drawing him in was equally repellent: a snake around his ribcage, threatening to squeeze all sense out of him. She wasn't here to stay; she'd be on that flight before he knew it; he'd been sure to remind himself of that—and her too—in case *this* moment ever arrived.

Another moment where he wanted to kiss her.

'So what happens now?' she asked him on a sigh. 'They got dragged off that ship pretty fast.'

He cleared his throat, pulled his eyes away with his hand. 'They'll scour the trawler for illegal trade, then the guys will likely wind up in jail. All *we* can do is go to Española at dawn, check for damages. If they made it onto land too, who knows what we'll find?'

'What about Aayla?'

'She'll stay here, with Dee.'

'But this is Dee's trip…why don't I stay with Aayla?'

Her offer danced in his mind, giving him a headache. Fixing his eyes on the black horizon he shook his head. No way was he leaving Aayla alone with Ivy, not even in these circumstances. The kid was getting attached enough as it was to someone who was leaving the second her honeymoon—or whatever this was—was over.

'We might need the both of us,' he said instead, measuredly. 'Like I told you, who knows what we'll find once we make land?'

Ivy sighed through her nose and the guilt rendered him silent, swigging his tea till it burned.

She'd leaped in to help tonight, literally, without him even asking. She'd shown no fear at all when they'd been slashing those nets. She'd probably saved a thousand marine lives alongside him in the blink of an eye. Without her help, it might have been a different story. He bit down hard on his tongue, wishing he could shake the need to tell Ivy how grateful he was that she'd been there. But he couldn't find the words. Didn't want to hear them from his own mouth. Already she was settling under his skin, like an itch he couldn't scratch. He'd needed her just now…a tourist, no less.

'Are you OK?' Ivy stood from the chair and crouched in front of his. 'You seem anxious. You did everything you could, Jero. They caught those guys because of you. Aayla is fine. She thinks you're a hero.'

He watched her lips, and only half heard her words. Just one slight movement and he could pull her in, scoop one hand behind her head again and claim her mouth this time. She'd been giving him the signs all day. He'd felt her fingers clawing his shirt earlier like feeling his clothes wasn't enough, felt her eyes on him ever since they'd boarded this boat. He could have her straddling him right here on this chair, let her melt into him under the moon. It was very clear she wanted it too, even if she wasn't doing anything about it.

For good reason. Get a hold of yourself, man.

He stood, left her on her haunches by his chair, while he busied his fingers with screwing the lid back onto the flask. 'You should get some sleep,' he grunted, turning away so she wouldn't see how much this deplorable desire was unsettling him.

'I'll wake you up at first light.'

CHAPTER EIGHT

IVY'S NERVES HAD been shot all morning, since before they'd ridden out here in the little Zodiac boat, leaving Aayla and Dee behind on the larger boat. They were still waiting for news on what—if anything—had been found on the seized trawler besides fish but thankfully Jero had been wrong about them coming ashore, too.

She watched the ticcing motion of his strong jaw as he scanned the beach for injured wildlife, as if he didn't quite believe their luck. The wind tussled at their clothes. She was already having to squint through the drizzle.

'You must have seen the results of a previous island swipe, from the look on your face,' she ventured aloud, hugging her arms around herself.

'You don't even want to know what they'll do, once they decide what they want,' he replied stoically. 'Why do you think that young orphaned penguin followed me home, that time?'

Ivy swallowed.

The rain was picking up speed and strength by the second, soaking her clothes. Jero's T-shirt was almost transparent. Every muscle cast another shadow under the grey sky. He'd hardly spoken all morning and she was trying not to wonder if the night's events were the only reason.

He'd gone cold on her pretty quickly last night; drifted away like a glacial front, just when she'd got a glimpse inside his head. *Men,* she'd huffed, when he'd gone. It was preferable to be more annoyed than hurt after all. She'd pretty much called him a hero. Big mistake. Yes, Aayla had said it first, but if he thought she was going to gush over him too, only to be ignored...

'Ivy. Over there.'

She followed his finger just as Jero made for another sea lion pup further up the beach. This one was alone, writhing on the sand, bellowing out little helpless honks that splintered her heart. She crouched at his side to inspect the creature. It was bigger than the last, roughly the size of a medium-sized dog.

'It doesn't look hurt,' she observed. 'Just a little malnourished.'

Ivy saw her reflection in its big, round sorrowful eyes. 'Where did your mama go?' she whispered, stroking a hand along the animal's smooth, almost waxy fur. Usually they weren't supposed to touch the wildlife here, but as a vet, and a woman, some maternal instinct to protect these creatures was quickly taking over. Whatever their species, babies needed caring for.

'Looks like the mother's abandoned him for some reason. It happens,' Jero said wanly. 'Maybe her mother couldn't feed herself and couldn't produce the milk to feed her.'

His jaw twitched again, and she wondered if he thought about his ex whenever he saw a lonesome creature looking around for its long-gone mother, the same way she thought about herself as a kid, sitting on the floor under the stairs reading *The Hungry Caterpillar* to Zeus.

'What can we do?' she asked as the goose-bumps prickled up on her arms. The rain and the intensity of this situation were making her colder by the second.

He sighed, offering her a sideways glance. 'The National Park vet would usually see about a bottle-feeding situation, but she can't leave the island and we don't have the facilities to maintain that here.'

To her surprise, he put a hand to the back of her neck under her hair. Instinctively she leaned in for just a second as his thumb made a small comforting circling motion on her skin. The gesture sent a solar flare directly to her loins in spite of their situation. A sob she'd somehow managed to contain since their rescue last night welled in her throat, and she only just managed to swallow it back again.

'Good thing Aayla's not here. She might have tried to carry it back to the boat in her backpack anyway,' he mused.

Ivy didn't trust her own voice now. She might've tried the same thing once. For all the good they did here, they couldn't help every animal. It just made her want to stay longer, try harder. Do more. Suddenly she understood why Jero had arrived here all these years ago and never left.

Flipping back to vet mode, Jero handed her a notebook and pen from his backpack. 'Make a note of the physical characteristics, his size, external earflaps, fur colour…we have to report every animal we come across…'

They worked together for an hour in the rain, carefully scouring the beach for any birds, sea lions and iguanas displaying signs of distress. The only thing that looked distressed, however, was Jero. Was he still thinking about the sea lion pup, or was it Aayla? He probably felt bad for scaring her last night, but the kid was tough. Once she'd learned that they were trying to stop tonnes of marine life from meeting their untimely death, her little fists had balled up and her mouth had twisted at the injustice. She hadn't looked upset, she'd been angry.

Ivy barely knew the kid, but she could see the way Aayla cared for her animals. She'd helped to shield her young eyes from some kind of massacre last night but, at the time, she hadn't even realised what she was doing. Did she really jump on that lifeboat, before Jero even had a chance to?

They made their way back down the winding coastal path towards the Zodiac boat and Ivy focused on his backpack ahead, thinking about Aayla and what he'd said last night, about losing her. It was pretty clear he did still carry the scars from his ex abandoning them, just as she still panicked inside whenever she pictured someone else she loved leaving *her*.

Maybe that was partly why she'd left Simon, before he could leave her, she wondered absently for the first time ever. One of them was probably always going to go eventually, even if she *had* agreed to bear his children. It was awful to think about, yes, but facts were facts. They'd just never really had all that much in common. She should have woken up years before the kids thing forced her to. When did she decide that, just because she'd been ignored before, she'd have to settle for the first man who paid her a little attention?

'Not far to go now. You OK back there?' Jero cut into her thoughts, turning back over his shoulder. His shirt was fully plastered to his form now in the rain, like some kind of island sculpture.

'All good,' she replied, glancing down at her own rain-soaked shirt. The pale minty green and white stripes were kind of see-through already. Had he noticed?

She rolled her eyes to the grey sky—what did it matter how she looked for him? Why was she letting this man confuse her like this? Rather than admit they might have something in common last night, Jero had pushed her away. The way his tone had changed when he'd asked her: *'So, when is your flight out of here again?'* It still made her shiver.

She really *should* check when her flight was, though. Mike was probably dying to have her back…or not. He hadn't called in a while, now that she thought about it. She was getting a little concerned he might be worried about telling her he wanted to sell.

The more they stalled, the more they were offered for the clinic in its prime location, but they could only buy so much time. Mike had a family to raise; the money would mean he could take a few years out from work to enjoy that, but what would *she* do? It wasn't about the money to her. It wasn't about having a man either; she would always need to feel needed.

'How did you know this was what you wanted to do? Live out here, I mean. Caring for all these wild creatures, especially in situations like this?' she asked Jero as they hurried onwards.

'It's not all paradise, like the tourists think,' he replied, clambering over a fallen log and stopping to check she made it, too. The sandy ground was flooded in places now, and lava lizards scurried from their path as they forged ahead.

'On my second day here, when the last surgical light burned out, I had to use a headlamp in surgery for the rest of the week.'

'A headlamp? Really?' Ivy swept a branch out of her face as leaves and thorns threatened to take her out. The action caused a shower of stored-up rain to soak her hair even more.

'That's island life,' he said. He lifted the next branch away from her face so she could make it underneath it safely. 'When a family's dog was knocked down by a car in my first month here, we didn't even have a splint for its broken leg. I had to go to two local hardware stores. Even then, all I could find that would work was some window trimming. It was stiff enough after they cut it to size for me.'

'Did it heal?'

'The dog was fine. But that's when I realised there was more that I could do here on these islands than I could ever do anywhere else. That's when I went about setting something up permanently. There's still so much to do, but we don't have to go to the hardware store for makeshift splints any more, so that's something.'

He held another branch back for her. 'I like how no day is the same, but still, we make a difference.'

'I kind of like your island life,' she said, before she could even register the words exiting her own mouth. 'On days like this, I wish I didn't have to leave.'

Jero stopped in his tracks and turned to her. Her heart lurched as he reached for her face and produced a stray leaf. It must have been caught in her hair. The rain seemed to disappear. Everything disappeared. Her fingers found his hand as it hovered close to her cheek with the leaf… just as a crash of thunder shook the sky and the heavens burst open.

She shrieked. Jero clamped her hand in his and started running. She could barely see where they were going now through the torrent of rain lashing at her face, but suddenly he was urging her towards a makeshift shelter, a box of sorts, which seemed to be made of several wooden upright planks and a straw-covered roof. She found herself inside the tiny enclosure, panting, catching her breath as Jero pushed open a tiny window at eye level, sending a shaft of light in.

'It's for the birdwatchers,' he explained, and Ivy laughed nervously, dropping to a tiny seat as the rain crashed against the roof like bullets. Dry moss and leaves were scattered across the floor. Somewhere, an unseen animal scurried away.

Jero dropped the backpack to the ground. The shelter seemed to shrink to fit them both. 'Are you sure you don't want to leave?' he asked her now, motioning skywards to the torrential rain with a wry smile, shaking out his arms and shirt.

Ivy hugged her arms around herself, watching the manta on his arm in the beam of light. 'I don't know,' she told him, truthfully. Jero, standing here before her like some kind of hunter warrior on this windswept, rain-soaked four-million-year-old island was turning her heart into a dancing circus monkey. Being in a bird-watching box didn't help.

'We both know you *have* to leave,' he said pointedly, inching closer to her still.

'I know,' she managed, lifting her head to meet his gaze, letting her hands close the gap between them, till her fingers were clasping at the hem of his T-shirt. 'I do have to leave eventually, but...'

What was happening to her brain? Every word they were exchanging felt like some kind of nail into a coffin. His eyes were glimmering with desire; he felt it too, this *thing*. Right now, in this moment, two very different lives were merging before her, throwing her off-kilter. Part of her wanted to stay longer, making sure nothing like the horror show out there ever happened again. Helping him.

Helping *herself* to *him*...who was she kidding?

A reckless kind of energy surged inside her.

Ivy pulled him in as if her life depended on it. Jero reciprocated, sweeping down to claim her lips like a wild creature swooping for its prey. Her tummy dissolved into a warm, liquid ball of lust as their kiss deepened and intensified like the rain pounding the straw roof above their heads.

His voice came hard and terse, setting her heart alight. 'Ivy.'

A fizzing current tore through her veins as he pulled her up from the seat to him, igniting every fibre of her being. She squished the voice as it scorned her: *You shouldn't be doing this... you've been staying away from this for good reason, too many reasons to count...*

His lips seared hers possessively. His tongue swirled and ravished her mouth in a hungry dance. She never could have guessed it could feel like this. That she could be this turned on by a relative stranger. *Shocking...but, oh, yes... more!*

A deep moan of pleasure escaped her open mouth as she found herself clasping the bulk of his muscled shoulders. Muscles rippled in her hands. *He's so freaking hot.*

Jero slowed his kiss, and his fingers trailed a pattern up her ribcage to the hem of her bikini top, lifting her wet shirt as he went, making her physically ache for him.

Her breath came sharp as her nipples stiffened. The feel of him caressing the curve of her breast like precious treasure—it was enough to make her damp in places the rain couldn't reach.

Dizzily she melted like butter against him, then gasped in anticipation as his other hand swept her head back, finding fistfuls of her hair at the nape of her neck. His lips rained kisses across her shoulder blades, her mouth and breasts. She'd dreamed of this after all, while wishing the thoughts away, and now, tasting his kiss, reality was a thousand times better.

You're going to fall for him now...what an idiot move this is. Her ego tried to chastise her again, but she shushed it away, arched her back and pressed into him, dying for more.

Then, as if to tease her or torment her, Jero withdrew his perfect mouth, pulled back an inch and trailed a thumb across her bottom lip, gazing so deep into her eyes that a shiver shook through her, not from the cold this time.

'I've been thinking about doing that for days.' His mouth curled in a half-smile that quickly turned to something like faint admonishment as he caressed her face with one big hand. 'I've been telling myself not to.'

She gaped at him, too dazed to utter a word. She needed to feel his lips on hers again before regret took hold of her too. She wanted this moment to last, way too much to talk. Reaching a hand to the back of his head, she pulled him in again, caressing his shaven scalp, tracing his tattoo with her other hand.

His ebony eyebrows drew together. 'See what you're doing to me,' he half growled, half purred against her mouth, and she shut him down with another kiss. The sensual sound of his enjoyment sent new bolts of anticipation rippling through her. She could feel what she was doing to him; it was pressed firm against her thigh as he found her lips again.

'I'm safe,' she heard herself saying, finding the zip on his shorts, kissing him deeply as he shook them aside. She hadn't stopped taking her pill.

Jero murmured something indecipherable, then cupped her backside and lifted her off the floor, placing her back on the tiny seat. Instinctively, her legs wrapped tight around his waist. His hardness made her damper than ever and when he pushed her underwear aside it took just one thrust for him to slide inside her. She was so ready.

His fingers twined into her hair. Arching her head back, he took her lips again and she forgot where she was completely as he thrust in and out, hard and swift, softly and slowly, filling her up deeper every time. Oh, God!

Deep unrivalled pleasure coursed through her with every move. Every hot, wet stroke and slide took her further into delirious, delicious insanity and she hugged his middle with her legs, feeling her climax building already. The wildness of it had every atom in her body throbbing and pulsating. *This* was the hottest sex she'd ever had!

Time was an alien concept suddenly. They could have spent minutes there, or hours, she couldn't get her brain around anything but the feel of him. When she toppled over the edge of pleasure, crying out into his mouth with the contractions, Jero jerked inside her. His expression sharpened to such fierce intensity as he came that her throat dried up. Together they shook and trembled with a new undoing, and Ivy struggled to find her breath. *What just happened?*

Jero collapsed against the wall, shaking his head. Laughter bubbled in her throat at the spent expression on his face; she felt so naughty, like a bad, bad schoolgirl with her boyfriend in the bike shed.

'The rain's stopped,' he observed after a moment, eyeing her warily as he pulled his shorts back on and scraped a hand across his head. She couldn't read him now, but every blood vessel was still tingling between her thighs. *Did we really just do that?*

Jero swept up his backpack from the ground and elbowed the door open. Sunlight flooded in, sending her crashing back to reality. The sky was blue again. Their path back to the boat was clear. She hadn't even noticed.

The boat ride back to their island was quiet. Ivy read a book, or at least pretended to. She kept sneaking glances at him. He looked distant, distracted. OK, so a lot had happened, and not just between them, but was he regretting that spontaneous sex? She didn't want to regret it, but if it meant things would be weird from now on, she would.

Ugh, maybe that was too reckless. Amazing,

yes. Unmatched in every way, but while it was probably inevitable that they'd act on this attraction somehow, she was the tourist here, just like his ex. Her presence, and this closeness, must stir up memories, remind him of what he'd lost before by doing the exact same thing. Was he putting her into the 'big mistake' box already?

She'd walked head first into a tricky situation, but it wasn't just her, was it? Discomfort snaked through her as he averted his eyes the second they found hers across the deck. They'd both crossed a line they couldn't go back from.

CHAPTER NINE

JERO WAS JUST walking into the clinic as Ivy exited the operating room. She caught his eye as she pulled off her surgical gloves and paused in her stride, probably surprised to see him. His stomach lurched with the eye contact as he dropped the box of syringes he was carrying down beside the desk, but she'd never know it, because he'd been doing pretty good at keeping his cool since the other day out on Isla Española.

'You're early,' she said, adjusting the bun of red curls piled high on her head. 'I thought you were out with the mobile clinic.'

'I was, and now I'm back. I have to restock before we head to Floreana later.'

He tapped the box of syringes and she frowned. 'I thought you'd wait for Aayla. She's finishing school in half an hour.'

'She's going on a playdate. I doubt she'll make it here today.'

'Oh. OK.' Ivy looked sideways. 'I haven't seen

her, or Pluma, not since we got back from Española.'

'Well, a lot has been going on,' he said as the guilt began to rage around his heart.

The huge black cat squirmed in their client's arms beside her. The short man holding it cleared his throat, looking between them in interest. 'If you don't mind, I should get going,' he said in Spanish.

Jero hurried to open the door for him at the same time as Ivy. They collided in the entrance and Ivy let out a harried sigh. He clocked her flushed cheeks; the way she shook out her arms, then straightened her white coat, all while avoiding his eyes. She was all wound up now, no thanks to his arrival. Or his lie. Could she tell he'd been keeping himself and Aayla at a distance as much as possible since his totally unacceptable, seemingly irrevocable crush got out of hand?

He swiped a hand across his head, knocking his sunglasses sideways and correcting them quickly. *Great job, Jero. So much for keeping it cool.*

'How did the surgery go?' he asked her when they were alone in Reception. Ivy made a thing out of writing something down in a folder he didn't recognise. She started telling him about the cat, and the urethrostomy, or penis amputation, she'd just performed on it due to the sixth urinary obstruction it had suffered in as many months. Watching her lips move took him back to the island…like most things she said now did.

It was very unfortunate. No matter how much he distracted himself he couldn't stop reliving how they'd almost brought the whole damn bird-watching box down with their antics. Man…he hadn't had sex like that in a long time; maybe ever. The way the trembles of her orgasm had rippled through him; that was some connection. He'd been craving the taste of her ever since…

'Jero?'

'What? Sorry, were you talking to me?'

Her amber eyes narrowed. 'I was saying how I've started a new filing system. It should make things a little easier for you all. Should we go over it now?'

His turn to frown now. 'Why did you do that?'

He stepped around the desk and flipped through the neatly labelled patient file, but she was opening the laptop, typing into some programme he also didn't recognise, ticking online boxes, telling him how they should log all their notes here too from now on.

'We don't do things like that,' he told her, shifting on his feet, feeling the lump of coal in his heart drop to his stomach and start to burn.

'Well, you should. It's better this way,' she retorted. 'You need a digital trail.'

'Why?'

'Because it's not 1963, Jero, and the world has moved on. I can't imagine why you're so offended by evolution. What would Darwin say, if he was still here?'

Jero clenched the insides of his cheeks. Changes were not things he particularly embraced, especially when they were initiated by someone who'd come in out of nowhere and messed with his head enough already.

'I don't want a digital trail, Ivy. It's more personal this way,' he said coolly. 'We know where everything is in the *real* world. Why fix what isn't broken?'

'Just give it a chance, will you?' She sighed. 'And I'm not sure you do know where everything is. You're always looking for files. It wastes time.'

He opened his mouth to respond but Ivy was already bashing something else into the computer, a fierce look of purpose on her face. OK, she had a point. His way of filing *was* pretty dated. And maybe it was more than her new filing system annoying him.

They'd both given into their attraction out there on the island. It wasn't all Ivy's fault that his carefully regulated world had just been twisted all out of alignment. He shouldn't have caved in as he had. All he'd done was invite more trouble into his life. Aayla's too. Ivy had cast her spell and burrowed under his skin, which was not a good place for her to be, seeing as she was leaving in just over a week.

He knew she was leaving. And he'd got his heart involved anyway.

'You put the animal's details in this column, and the contact details on this tab…'

He stood in silence as she explained the online system and tried to pay attention over the noise of a fresh litter of stray kittens Dudders had brought in earlier, mewing for attention in the back. This was just one more thing to think about in an endless list—he had to head back out with the mobile clinic in less than two hours, this time to Floreana.

He'd promised Dee an update on the trawler saga, which meant heading to her research base at the Tortoise Station up in the Santa Cruz highlands, where he'd also examine the giant tortoises for new pregnancies. A friend of Aayla's was coming to the house tonight with her mother, to see about adopting a puppy. Did he promise them dinner too? He couldn't even remember.

All he could think now was, why was Ivy

going out of her way to help him, when he'd been a total jerk?

Maybe she was just as mad at herself for complicating things, he considered now. *Neither* of them had addressed what had happened out there on Española yet. Instead, they'd been doing some awkward dance around each other ever since, like two courting albatrosses unsure of the next step. Sure, they were busy, but not too busy to have found the time to talk by now.

Maybe they *did* need to talk about it. He should let her know where she stood so she didn't expect anything more while she was here.

Yes, he would tell her that. That way he'd draw a line for himself too. A very distant line from any further temptation...which, come to think of it, was probably why he'd been avoiding her in the first place. Distance meant he couldn't get any closer, even though he wanted to.

Smart, Jero. But not exactly fair.

He flipped the lid down on the laptop, left his hand on top.

'Ivy, about what happened. We should probably...'

Relief flooded her eyes. 'Oh, God, yes, Jero. I was thinking the same thing...'

She swivelled the chair to him, inviting conversation, but the doorbell jingled an interruption and in walked their next client with

Bernardo, a huge brown and white dog the size of a Shetland pony.

Ivy tore her eyes from his and stood, while all the words he'd been planning to say dissipated in the air conditioning. They both plastered smiles to their faces. Jero cursed the timing under his breath.

What was she thinking, exactly? What did she think he was going to say? Why did he care so much, dammit?

His phone rang on the desk, stealing the moment completely.

Aayla's school.

His heart sank like a ship even before the teacher spoke. Aayla had gone outside to the bathroom ten minutes ago and she hadn't come back yet. They couldn't find her. He stared blankly at the wall a second, processing it. Every father's nightmare.

Ivy must have sensed the slow-building dread in the pit of his stomach or seen it on his face.

'What's wrong?'

'Aayla's missing.' He could barely believe the words coming from his own mouth.

'Missing?'

'Can you handle this examination?' he asked her.

'Of course I can handle it.' She put a hand to his arm. 'Go!'

He didn't miss the concern that flickered in her eyes before he turned for the door, but he couldn't take it onboard. He couldn't even contemplate that she might have something to worry about.

'She won't have gone far, try not to worry!' she called after him.

Jero bit his tongue the whole way to Rainbow Grove Primary School, as if he might yell his real thoughts to the trees along the sandy path if he didn't. It was a fifteen-minute walk usually, but now he was running, his head a blur. So much for not contemplating that there might be a real problem; his phone was still silent. Which meant no one had seen her yet.

'Aayla!' His voice carried on the breeze, disturbing a chicken pecking the path ahead, and two tourists wielding cameras and giant backpacks.

What if she'd been kidnapped, stolen right off school property?

What if one of those fishermen from the illegal trawler had come to exact revenge? Of course, they probably wouldn't recognise him, or her. They were still incarcerated anyway, awaiting trial as far as he knew.

But what if…what if…what if…?

Telling him not to worry just proved how little Ivy knew him, or anyone else who was trying to be the best parent for their child. You worried all the time. There was barely a moment when you didn't worry. You could worry all damn day and all night if you stopped to think about the dangers your child might inadvertently wander into on the path of life, all while you were looking the other way.

Not that Ivy had any real reason to know that, he reminded himself. She hadn't known much in the way of parenting. She'd barely been around a child before meeting Aayla.

He admonished himself, kicking a pebble in his path and apologising to a sleeping dog as it landed in front of his nose and woke him up. There he was again, being hard on *Ivy*, when really he *should* be being harder on himself. Ivy had been nothing but great for Aayla so far; the rest was in his head. A result of his own guilt over upsetting the status quo, which could in turn, if he wasn't more careful, upset Aayla.

Aayla could pick things up from a mile away, every bit of chemistry and tension. She knew something was up with him and Ivy, now that he thought about it. She'd been adamant that Ivy read to her on the boat, and she'd been asking to hang out with her ever since their return.

He'd told her no, kept her just as busy as him on other things…but he wasn't proud of himself for it.

'Did you find her?' Concern and fear had become a bubbling geyser waiting to erupt by the time the kindly middle-aged Ecuadorian woman, Mrs Ferdinand, took him aside outside the school gates.

It was home time. All around him, parents were collecting their kids and the hot sticky air was thick with laughter and high-pitched chatter. The friendly community he'd seen grow around him and Aayla had never made him feel so alone.

'We still haven't seen her,' Mrs Ferdinand apologised, as Angie, the single mother of Aayla's planned playdate, approached, looking just as worried. 'But we think she must have gone looking for her bird somewhere.'

'Pluma?' Jero scratched his head, pulling his silent phone out again, as if some random, kind stranger might call him if he watched the screen, and report that they'd found her. Perspiration built at the back of his neck, and he fanned out his shirt. Angie bit her bottom lip, eyeing him up and down.

'She's made quite a name for herself in this place, with that bird,' the principal told them.

Angie squeezed his arm and he pulled it away. 'Apparently, she started to try and fly in the classroom, and Aayla got quite upset about it. We think it might have happened again when they were outside...'

'Is anyone looking for them?' Angie asked.

'Of course, every teacher and volunteer, some of the parents too—'

'She doesn't do this. She doesn't just wander off,' he interrupted, heading off alone towards the rainbow-painted outhouse where she was last seen, calling her name. Desperation was making an empty well of his stomach. He hit the beach next. Was it too soon to call the authorities? To make sure no one left the island until she was found?

He called to check, jarred by the wobble in his own voice. They were already on it, of course—the school had alerted them. It made the silence of his phone seem louder.

For the next hour Aayla's name echoed all around him as others joined the search. From the beach to the street, people were gathering, talking, hypothesising under their breath no doubt, all looking for his daughter. It was all Jero could do not to sink to the sand and rock himself into a parallel universe; one where this was not happening.

CHAPTER TEN

'NAYELY?' IVY PRESSED the phone to her ear over the squall of the seabird someone had just deposited in reception. It hadn't been too injured by the child's wayward football to forget how to bring a house down, and the noise wasn't exactly soothing her frenzied mental process. 'Zenon!' she called to the storeroom. 'Zenon, in here, please!'

She'd been worrying about Aayla, and Jero ever since Jero had left over an hour ago. Now Nayely was calling from the hotel reception. *Please, no,* she thought, signalling for Zenon to take the bird with him into the back. Now was not the time to learn her room had flooded, or the ceiling had caved in, or worse.

'Ivy, I think you need to come here. I can't get hold of Jero.'

Ivy's stomach contracted. 'What?'

'Aayla is here. She's asking for you.'

* * *

Within minutes, Ivy had left Zenon fully in charge of the squawking flightless cormorant and hurried back across town on the bicycle loaned to her by Aqua Breeze Couples' Resort. She'd never ridden it so fast.

Swinging through the hotel doors to the lobby, she found Nayely sitting with a tear-stained Aayla on the purple plush sofa, snuggling Pluma to her chest. It was quite a sight: a child and a bird with blue feet. A couple wheeling suitcases, who looked to be in their sixties, cooed and ventured closer on their way past, but Aayla spotted her and leapt to her flip-flopped feet.

'Ivy!'

To her shock the kid ran for her across the marble floor and Pluma tried her best to ruffle her feathers. She couldn't quite manage, seeing as Aayla now had a firm grip on her soft feathered body.

'Jero's on his way. I finally got hold of him,' Nayely told her, glancing behind her.

The poor woman had a queue of people to attend to now, but it seemed she'd held them off. They were all drinking some kind of cocktail, watching Pluma, looking nothing but amused. Ivy thanked her profusely for not leaving Aayla's side. What a community they had here! She dropped to the sofa in relief while Aayla babbled on at her, talking a million miles an hour in both Spanish and English.

'This was where you found her, Ivy. Maybe Pluma wanted to fly to you?'

'Well… I never thought about that,' she said truthfully.

'I wish we had your camera when she flew.' Aayla stood between Ivy's knees, and Ivy prised the bird gently from her hands, setting her on her lap. She tried to keep her voice calm and collected.

'She flew, already?'

'She tried to fly away!' Aayla's lip wobbled. Then she started to cry again. 'What if she doesn't love me any more?'

Ivy felt her throat dry up.

'Don't cry, sweetie,' she managed, looking all around for help. It was deeply uncomfortable hearing her cry. Suddenly she knew why. It took her back to all the times *she'd* cried, alone, convinced that her own mother would rather be anywhere than at her side. Some kind of strange maternal instinct to protect her kicked in again, as it had done back on the boat when she'd kept on slashing those nets, knowing if they didn't break she'd present this poor kid with a sight she'd never be able to un-see.

'Did you actually see Pluma fly?' Ivy asked

her softly, right before Nayely called across the
lobby to confirm that, yes, Pluma had flown to
the hotel entrance and tried to get in by pecking
at the door. Aayla had appeared moments later,
claiming Pluma had landed several times along
the path here from the school. It sounded a lot
as if the tame bird had been checking to make
sure Aayla was following her.

Unbelievable, Ivy mouthed. The bird was a
miracle. This was the first she'd heard of Pluma
flying, but it surely wouldn't be the last. Jero's
words came back to her: how you couldn't keep
anything with wings anywhere it didn't want
to be.

Ivy got to her knees in front of the child,
wiped the tears from her cheeks with her fingers as she'd seen her friends do to their children. It wasn't as awful as she'd previously
expected. Aayla calmed down instantly, which
sent a strange rush of warmth to her heart and
somehow comforted her, too.

'She's a wild creature, Aayla,' she told her
gently. 'She's going to fly sometimes. But it
sounds like she came to a place she thought one
of us would be. And she brought you here too!
That means she loves us both, does it not?'

The sobbing Aayla seemed to contemplate
this for a second, while Ivy realised the truth
of her own words. Pluma *must* feel a bond with

both of them, if she'd come here to Aqua Breeze. She'd rescued her from the beach just outside.

'She's going to miss you!' Aayla sniffed, making the liquid comfort blanket dissolve from her heart on the spot. But then, Aayla embraced her in a huge hug, almost squishing poor Pluma between them again.

'Aayla?' They sprang apart. Jero was here, flying through the double doors towards them, scooping Aayla up in his arms. 'Aayla, you scared me to hell and back. What are you doing *here*?'

Ivy stood slowly, registering how her pulse had sounded in her ears the second he'd appeared.

'I'm sorry, Daddy, I was looking for Pluma. But Pluma was looking for Ivy.'

For a second, as he held her and checked her face for scratches, and asked if she was OK, Ivy felt completely invisible. This was a pure father-daughter moment, in which anyone could see, without a shadow of a doubt, how much Aayla meant to Jero.

She found herself blinking back tears as some kind of new, gut-based longing possessed every part of her. Longing for what? She didn't quite know. It had started just now, when Aayla said Pluma would miss her.

Maybe she was destined never to be a part of

something this important. Maybe she'd never know this kind of love. She'd always been too busy telling herself she didn't want it. What was wrong with her?

'Ivy?'

She shook herself, dashing a hand across her eyes. Jero was talking to her, asking her something about the clinic. 'Zenon's there,' she answered quickly, annoyed at herself for getting emotional. 'Pluma flew here, Jero…'

'I know,' he said, finally releasing his daughter. His hand found hers, and just his touch sent a shockwave up her arm. 'Thank you for handling things so fast.' His voice was a gentle, warming breeze in her ear. 'My phone was all choked up with other people calling to see if I'd found her.'

Before she could respond he strode across the lobby to Nayely. 'I can't thank *you* enough either.'

'I didn't really do anything,' Nayely started, but Ivy watched her neat black eyebrows rise to the roof as Jero swept her in and hugged her so hard the poor woman floundered, clearly shocked by his enthusiastic embrace.

'These women, both of them, are extraordinary!' he enthused vociferously to the line of cocktail-drinking couples waiting to check in or out. Everyone applauded; some even whistled. The sixty-something woman giggled under her

Galapagos visor like a schoolgirl. Her husband cocked a greying eyebrow in sudden suspicion, crossing his arms over his booby T-shirt.

Ivy bit back a smile at the sight of Nayely's flushed cheeks. Maybe she wasn't the only one with a crush on Jero around here. Not that Nayely, or this sweet retiree, had ever wrapped their legs around him in a birdwatching box, in the middle of a rainstorm.

What are you doing to yourself, Ivy?

She forced her eyes away, gathered up her bag from the sofa. Now was not the time to revisit their hot one-day stand or wish it would happen again. Jero had avoided being alone with her ever since, so clearly he regretted it too. Wasn't that what he'd been about to tell her earlier? That he wanted to forget it ever happened? She'd been expecting that, so of course she'd been ready to agree.

Obviously he wanted no part of a 'fling' with a tourist. She'd known that much before they let their impulses take over out on that island, and that was fine by her. *She* didn't do flings either. She was, as Mike liked to say, an all-or-nothing kind of woman. More nothing than all, most of the time, but still. What did she have to offer *these* people, really?

This was their little bubble, their inner circle. Their family.

* * *

'I'm supposed to be on Floreana by now, with the mobile clinic.' Jero scowled, scanning his phone when they were outside on the hotel driveway.

She put a hand to his arm. 'Cancel it, we'll go tomorrow. You've just had a pretty intense couple of hours—take some time out.'

Beside them, Pluma was waddling on the sand under Aayla's watchful gaze. Jero had given her a strict instruction in the lobby not to try and hold her back. *If Pluma wants to fly, let her fly.'

'OK, but I should still go and see Dee at the Tortoise Station,' he mused aloud to a nearby tree, sliding his phone back into his pocket and making the sexy cryptic manta on his arm come to life for just a second in the sun.

'Tomorrow,' she repeated. Why was he so stubborn? The man had more things on the go than her and that was saying something.

Jero let out a sigh. 'OK, but I think I promised to cook dinner for one of Aayla's friends and her mom. They're coming to pick out a puppy.'

Ivy closed her mouth. She'd been about to protest this plan, too, but she did want to see the puppies get rehomed. Jero had taken them all in as fosters while they looked for new families for them.

'Can Ivy come for dinner, Daddy?' Aayla

tugged at the bottom of Jero's shirt, casting her big brown eyes up from her to Jero and back again. 'Pluma wants us all there. If we're all in one place, maybe she won't fly away again?'

'Oh, no, I, I'm busy...' Ivy trailed off, glancing at Jero. He wouldn't want her at their home, would he? Besides, she had to close up the clinic, finish adding the patient information to the new system, check in with Mike...because he hadn't exactly been forthcoming with his recent thoughts on the acquisition in her absence.

She was starting to get nervous. There were huge changes ahead if he wanted to sell and she decided not to...

'Sure, she can come for dinner, if she'd like,' Jero said, blowing all her other thoughts out of the window. He glanced at her sideways and shrugged before pulling his sunglasses over his eyes, rendering him unreadable. 'We wouldn't want to upset Pluma.'

Aayla let out a whoop as if it were a done deal, then gripped Ivy's hand like a vice, beckoning Pluma to follow them on her little blue feet up the pathway, the opposite way to the clinic. Ivy almost expected the bird to fly away again, but she seemed content with her previous adventure for now. Instead, she fluttered up to Jero's shoulder and perched there. The disbelief on her face must have made Jero laugh, and all tension was lifted. But through the hotel window, Ivy saw Nayely still watching them all, pretending not to.

'She wants a ride on Daddy!' Aayla exclaimed, bouncing up and down.

Who doesn't? Ivy thought to herself, feeling the anxiety creep back in again like a toxic jellyfish tentacle up her spine. If she went to their house, she and Jero might be forced to finish their conversation from earlier and talk about what happened. He'd tell her it could never happen again and while she'd have to agree... Ugh. Awkward.

She pushed the thoughts aside as they walked as a trio, with a bird, into the late afternoon sun. Nope. *Not today, insecurities.* She was a grown woman, and he a grown man. If he could do this, so could she.

This evening, and really the rest of her limited time here, was reserved for her duties. And adorable Aayla and Pluma, and the puppies. That was all.

CHAPTER ELEVEN

JERO FELT THE twisty tangle of what he now called Poison Ivy reclaim its grip on him, just at the sight of her administering a simple anaesthetic to the dog on the table before them. Not that Ivy Malone was anything but a remedy, but pretending he felt nothing in the face of her imminent departure was excruciating.

'Almost there, little guy,' she soothed as the adopted male street dog succumbed to the drugs, all ready for sterilisation. The truth was, Jero felt a little as though a part of himself were going under the knife, too.

Ivy was all checked out of the Aqua Breeze Couples' Resort. Her suitcase sat in the storeroom like some harbinger of doom, all ready for her to leave straight from here, straight to the ferry that would take her to the airport.

For days now, since *before* the dinner at his house, when Aayla had insisted Ivy be the one to tuck her and Pluma in and read them a story, he'd been holding back the burning urge to tell her that her being here had meant the world. To both of them.

It was always on the tip of his tongue. But he hadn't said a word.

They both knew what that encounter had been, right? A simple one-off. A very, very pleasurable, memorable one-off, but a one-off all the same. Getting all mushy and emotional about her leaving would feel too serious, too dramatic.

Or maybe telling her would feel too much like admitting he sort of liked having her around, that he needed her.

He didn't *need* her, not in the clinic, not anywhere. He'd fought too hard to get over the last tourist who'd sucked him in, and *married* him, then spat him out, and finally he was fine. No way was he going through that again, or anything remotely similar.

He'd let every single opportunity to talk to Ivy about anything non-trivial pass him by, and now it felt too trite to bring it up. Ivy hadn't tried to talk about what happened, either. If she was embarrassed or regretful about hooking up with someone else on her would-be honeymoon, he didn't know, but between them they'd mastered small talk instead of anything serious. And now, here they were. Counting down the minutes they had left…sterilising another animal.

'Pass me that knife?'

'He's looking pretty good to me.'

'Let's call his human. He'll be awake soon.'

Just tell her, Jero. Just say something nice. It's the least you can do.

That night when she'd joined them for dinner, Angie, Aayla's friend's mother, had done her usual chatterbox thing all night, from openly discussing her ex-husband's affairs at the dinner table, to picking out the plumpest, cutest puppy, to getting more than tipsy while Aayla and her daughter played upstairs.

When she'd finally departed, leaving him and Ivy alone in the house, he'd been about to bring their misadventures up casually again, in a no-big-deal kind of way, so at least they weren't just ignoring what had happened. But he couldn't quite think of how to say it. Then Aayla had called them up to her room for a story. Then Ivy had made some excuse to go home before she'd even made her way back down the stairs.

Maybe it was better this way?

Idiot. You'd rather just let her go now without a word, than actually talk about your feelings?

Of course, being Ivy, she'd insisted on coming in for her shift before leaving, so whatever it was between them that hadn't gone away simply because he'd hoped it might still lingered between them like an impertinent ghost.

* * *

It was still there in the car, two hours later.

'You know, you really didn't have to drive me to the ferry,' she said. Her hands were clenching and unclenching the bottom of her seat. Her jeans and brown leather boots, all ready for landing in Galway, only served to emphasise what different worlds they really lived in. He gripped the pick-up's steering wheel, then cut the engine. The car park was busy. The next solar-powered ferry to Baltra Airport was just pulling in.

'I'll come in with you,' he said, catching her eye in the mirror.

'Making sure I actually leave, huh?' she joked, clicking off her seat belt. But it probably wasn't really a joke. There wasn't anything particularly light about this moment; in fact, he was disturbed by the perpetual ache at his core. He didn't want to acknowledge it one bit, but he couldn't ignore it now.

He let her out of the car, let his hand linger too long on the small of her back as he wheeled her suitcase onto the ferry. They made the short crossing over the Itabaca Channel in relative silence under cloudy, moody skies, and the silence dragged on into Departures.

'Wow, it's busy in here,' she noted needlessly, rubbing at her arms, glancing at him sideways.

Why could he not just say it? He'd loved having her around, he wished she could stay longer. That one-off had left him wanting her more than he'd ever wanted anyone!

Why was he such a damn selfish, broken idiot?

Aayla had worn her heart on her *My Little Penguin* sleeve this morning, hugging Ivy goodbye before school. Ivy had asked him if she could leave her camera with Aayla but he'd refused. He would buy his daughter her own camera. She'd looked pretty hurt at his refusal but presents—aka reminders—weren't necessary here. He hadn't wanted to let her say goodbye at all, really. Goodbyes meant pain and tears to Aayla, no thanks to Suranne. They did to him, too, he supposed, but this wasn't about him.

Was it? He contemplated it for half a second.

'You're kidding me?' Ivy was scowling up at the departure board now. 'My connecting flight from Guayaquil is cancelled. Of all the bad timings. They could have sent a text…'

She stopped talking, then rolled her eyes. 'I know, I know, island life. But seriously, why now?'

Her words made him laugh and he didn't even know why. Instant relief, maybe? She wasn't going anywhere, not yet anyway.

His mind spun at the change of plan as he followed like a Sherpa with her case to the check-in desk. She slapped down her Irish passport. 'I need to get to Galway.'

'Sorry, ma'am, there's been a technical difficulty. The airline has paused all flights.'

Jero listened in as the smartly dressed woman in a red bow tie explained how one of the airline's international crafts had experienced an engine failure—but only in *one* of its engines—and that they'd put her on the next flight, in five days' time. More or less.

Ivy did a good job of not appearing as annoyed as he knew she probably was, even when they were back in the car, heading back to Puerto Ayora.

'Five days till I can fly. More or less. What will I do till then? I can't go back to Aqua Breeze,' she said, fixing her eyes on the passing scenery. 'Even if they weren't fully booked a year in advance, I'm pretty sure my so-called honeymoon was nothing but trouble for poor Nayely.'

Jero frowned to himself. Maybe he was crazy but he was already one step ahead.

'You know, if you want to keep volunteering, we can put you up at the staff accommodation. It's not so bad, if you don't mind the odd Bob Marley song drifting through your windows at night.'

She turned to him and for a second he thought

she might flat out laugh in his face at the notion of prolonging their awkward time together. 'You want to put me in a room next to Dudders?'

He shrugged, but he couldn't help chuckling under his breath. 'I'm just saying, the offer of a room is there, whether you want to carry on working for us or not.'

'Why would I not?'

Jero fell silent, feeling her eyes drill into him. Her question was loaded. 'I guess...you might have decided you're over it,' he tested after a moment.

'Because we never talked about what happened?' Ivy exhaled long and hard next to him. When she spoke next, her voice broke like a glass, shooting shards straight through his hardened shell. 'It doesn't mean I'm over it, Jero. In fact, if you must know, when I saw that flight was cancelled, I felt a bit relieved.'

Was she serious?

Jero put his foot down. Ivy gasped and gripped the dashboard as he swerved and pulled the car over, leaving the engine running in a cloud of dust. 'Get out,' he instructed.

Ivy stuttered, clutching her bag to her. 'What?'

'Get out!'

Before she could say anything more, he was already out of the car, striding around to her side. He yanked the door open, just as she was placing one decidedly un-beach-suitable boot onto the sandy ground.

'I didn't want you to leave just yet either.' Inexorable surging started up in his loins till he was acting on autopilot. He took her face in his hands, and for a moment, as reality caught up with him, he pressed his forehead to hers, feeling days of pent-up emotions threaten to spill out of him. *To hell with it.*

'I shouldn't have ignored what happened. I should have said something. I'm an idiot.'

'So am I!'

'I haven't been able to get that day, or the taste of you, out of my head.'

Ivy clutched his shirt by the collar and pulled him close. 'God, me neither.'

Just the scent of her tore through his senses, driving him wild. He found her lips, fuelled by the same intensity as before in the storm. Ivy's hands were suddenly all over him, claiming and possessing him on the side of the road like some demon hitchhiker he couldn't get enough of. They were kissing so furiously she was sprawled against the bonnet of the car with one leg hooked around his middle before they came up for air, and only then it was at the insistence of a truck driver, honking at them, trying to get his wide, heavy load of supermarket goods past their car.

* * *

Within the hour they were wheeling Ivy's case into the pristine sparkly lobby at the Pelican Hill Apartments. 'We had these built just before our house was built,' he explained, calling for the elevator. 'I lived here with Aayla for a while after...' He trailed off. No need to get into the break-up with Suranne now. 'Mostly I rent them out to the tourists.'

Ivy touched her fingers to her lips as she looked around the lobby with its giant Galapagos marine life wall feature and palms in silver pots. 'You had them built? You mean, you own these?' Her hand slid up and down his arm, as if she couldn't bring herself to break contact. 'Why did I not know that?'

'I guess I never told you,' he said. He found himself smiling at her slightly swollen lips, how they'd felt on his again right as he'd been about to let her go. They'd stopped the car several times on the way here to explore different routes, mainly around each other's mouths. Whatever was going on right now was probably reckless, and clearly everything he'd told himself he *wouldn't* do...but he was trying not to care. Somehow the universe—or a faulty plane—had given him another chance. How could he ignore that?

He pulled her close in the elevator and kissed

her, feeling her melt into him all the way up to the fourth floor, where she pulled away quickly as the doors opened. Just in case.

'I'll put you in 401,' he said, swiping his card across the key lock. 'Don't worry, Dudders is on the second floor.'

'You have digital locks here? That's interesting,' she teased, trailing kisses along his tattoo up to his neck, making him forget what he was doing for a second. 'I'm surprised you don't have to write my name down in a giant fusty-smelling leather-bound book…'

'Oh, we'll do that, too,' he said, hoisting her up over his shoulder. She squealed and laughed and pretended to protest as he pushed her case inside with his foot and kicked shut the door behind them.

Lowering her to the bed, he leaned over her, trapping her with her hands above her head, pressed to the mattress. 'Now what?' he growled, hearing his own desire catching in his throat.

'Now what?' she replied, pulling him down to her. In seconds he was smothering her in kisses, letting his tongue continue its journey into even more delicious places around Ivy's milky white body. Smooth as Irish silk. Sure, he shouldn't be doing this, any more now than when they did it the first time. But something was different now. This time he literally couldn't stop. No logic or reason was enough to make him take his hands off her.

He slid off her ridiculous boots. The rest of their clothes were on the floor in seconds. They both knew the car had been the foreplay. It didn't take long before she was writhing naked against him, sucking, caressing, moaning the way she had that day with the rain coming down hard over their heads. He trailed his fingers along the smooth white flesh of her stomach as she arched her hips to meet him and pleaded for him to be inside her.

'You want me?' he teased, hovering at the edge of her.

'More than I should,' she breathed.

That was invitation enough. She cried out as he bucked into her with one swift, hungry stroke that made clamps of her fingers over his shoulders. 'Oh, yes…'

Nothing had ever felt so damned good to him in his whole life. He shut down the voices telling him he'd regret this. Nothing had changed at all! He was well aware of that. Ivy was still leaving. Just not yet. And would a little fun before she left for good *really* be so bad?

He had to stop before he came completely undone too soon, so he slowed his strokes, but Ivy was a force to be reckoned with. She rode him expertly almost into oblivion for a second time. It felt like hours they spent there, switching things up and around, trying things he couldn't even remember trying before; or maybe it was just different with her. They fitted, no one could deny it. Her slim frame felt precious, all small and trembling against his, but Ivy wasn't shy. She knew exactly what she wanted.

'Jero, please...'

'Please what?' he mouthed against her as she made an animalistic sound that turned him on more than any noise he'd ever heard, and pulled his lips to hers, then pressed her mouth to his shoulder, looping her arms around him. The sheets were soaked, the palm trees looked positively bashful outside the window at what they were witnessing.

'Please, please, please!'

'Tell me you wanted more of this, ever since last time,' he demanded, clenching his jaw, hovering at the edge of her again. He loved the look on her face, the sheer agony of the promise he was making, and not quite delivering. Whatever had come over him didn't feel quite like him; it was as if she'd unlocked another side of him, something raw he'd never explored, but wanted to. Again, and again.

'I wanted it. I want it.' Ivy half grinned, half gulped a huge breath, and tried to pull him back by the hips. He entered her again with the force she was begging for, memorising her face as the pleasure pulsed through her. She laughed huskily and wickedly, as though she couldn't believe the side of her he was bringing out either.

He couldn't get enough of the noises she made, or the way she shrieked with delight and curled her toes. She gripped the sheets either side of her, turning her knuckles white. By the time he felt his release he could have sworn he'd just been dancing with her soul in a whole different dimension.

'It really takes five days to repair a plane...' Ivy mused, some time later, rolling to her back and catching her breath. He turned to face her on the pillow, studying the flecks of sunlight in her eyes and the giveaway glow of her cheeks. Daylight was still streaming through the window straight onto their damp, slick bodies and crumpled sheets.

'Five days, more or less,' he reminded her, smoothing a stray red curl behind her ear, only to watch it bounce right back. 'Doesn't sound like it's the best plane, if they need to fly spare parts in over the best part of a week.'

'Or a specialist engineer?' She pretended to shudder. 'Maybe I dodged a bullet. Maybe we should just make the most of it. Unless...'

She paused. He could almost hear her think.

'Unless?' he encouraged, but he could already read her face.

'I mean, I'm still leaving, Jero.' She traced the manta ray on his arm with one gentle finger and sighed. Suddenly, the mood was dead.

He echoed her sigh at the ceiling, kicking the cotton sheet from the bed to allow more cool air across his naked body. 'I know.'

'So…this isn't really a good idea, is it?' she followed. Ivy's expression turned pained as he watched her dark red brows draw together. She stroked a finger to his cheek next and the warmth transferred straight to his heart. He got the feeling she was waiting for him to disagree, but how could he, when she was right? He'd done it again, let his animal instincts take over. Reality was slapping his red-hot face already.

Aayla had been all torn up about Pluma flying away, and Pluma was just a bird. The kid was scarred, no thanks to his failure to keep Suranne on the island long enough to help him raise her. He'd be an idiot if he went down that road again with someone else. Saying goodbye to Ivy again would be confusing as hell for him…her.

Her.

He shook himself, dragged a hand across his head. He liked this woman, a lot more than he'd been expecting to, but women came, and women went from his life and when this one left too, for the second time, Aayla would be tortured with questions he wouldn't be equipped to answer. What kind of message was he sending to his daughter?

'Jero?' Ivy narrowed her eyes. He wanted to kiss her again, go in for round two, but he also wanted to grab up his things and go. Let this *really* be the last time they saw each other.

She linked her fingers through his, and pressed his hand to the pillow between them, as if she could already feel him slipping away. Her imploring eyes made him forget everything else except how good it felt to be with her, but she'd said it first, right? This *was* a bad idea. If they kept this up, even for five days—more or less—he wouldn't be able to help involving Aayla. It would be even more complicated down the line.

'I don't regret what just happened,' he started, feeling the weight of his thoughts building up on his tongue. The words felt heavy and cold, like ice cubes crushing out the flames that had just been roaring between them for the best part of an hour. But if he didn't say them now, he never would. He turned to her. 'No regrets, Ivy Malone.'

'No regrets,' she agreed, curling her fingers tighter in his.

'But you're right, Ivy. It's not a good idea. This can't happen again. Maybe you should enjoy however many days you have left. You can stay here, of course, but forget about working with me. Go out, enjoy the islands, take more photos...'

She sat bolt upright, clutching the sheets to her chest. The hurt on her face rocked his core. He'd actually been testing her a little bit, he realised now, hoping she might argue, or confess that she wanted to make something work that didn't mean ending things for ever in five days.

'OK,' she said slowly, measuredly, as his heart pummelled his ribs like a boxer in a cage fight. 'I guess I can understand that, all things considered. Aayla considered.'

He clenched his fists around the sheets. Idiot, of course she didn't want to make anything work. What did he expect? That she'd turn around and announce she was selling her practice in Ireland for him and moving here? With him and Aayla? They weren't enough for her, just as they weren't enough for Suranne. Of course, he'd fallen for another headstrong ball of fire who'd end up doing nothing but burn him, and his daughter.

He forced himself not to reach for her as she left an Ivy-shaped patch of warmth and sunlight on the bed and stood up. Biting hard on his tongue, he stared as she turned fully naked to face him. Dear God, she was magnificent.

He couldn't recall the last time he'd wanted a woman so badly, but he'd been stupid enough already, getting involved like this. Not every plane would break, and no honeymoon lasted for ever.

Let her go. Just let her go.

She studied him a second, then reached for her clothes. 'I guess this is the last you'll see of me, then, Jero. It's over.'

CHAPTER TWELVE

THE RADIO CAUGHT her attention from its perch on Marsha's packed fish stall. Ivy stopped with her camera in the middle of snapping three giggling children playing with a ball just beyond the bustling market. The locals were starting to pay attention to the news broadcast too—something about a rare bird on another illegal ship, discovered just outside the Galapagos National Park, tied to the same group of people who'd run the illegal trawler.

Marsha called her over. 'Ivy! I haven't seen you around in the last few days, I thought you'd left.'

'Nope, still here.' Ivy pressed the lens cap back on her SLR camera. She'd been keeping a relatively low profile since she'd found herself stuck here three days ago, mostly because she didn't want to invite questions like this, that might lead on to talking about Jero. By now it was probably rare for people to see her out without him.

Marsha touched a fishy hand to her arm across Álvaro, the ever-vocal sea lion. 'I think his voice is needed, Ivy, as usual. People listen to Jero.'

She stepped around Álvaro and smoothed down her green sundress. 'What?'

Marsha explained how Jero was one of the people who'd been called to give evidence at the trial over on the mainland. It had been expedited thanks to the new arrests, the international news coverage, and the rare bird. 'I was there too,' Ivy found herself saying incredulously. 'I saw it all. Why didn't they call me?'

Marsha blinked at her and rested a hand on her trellis table, just missing a severed fish head with her fingers. 'I don't know. Ask them or ask Jero. Aren't you still working at the clinic?'

'Not exactly.' Ivy drew a deep breath and allowed the moment to be interrupted by the resident pelican as it made a swoop for the fish head. Marsha shooed it away, and Ivy took her leave.

In an instant she wanted to call Jero, but nope. She was not going to do that. Yes, it was a constant stab in the gut knowing she was so close, yet so far from him after everything that had happened. The more she let what happened replay in her head, the more panicky she felt about having overreacted. In her silence, in staying away, she was playing the role of the tourist who was always going to leave, instead of maybe... just maybe, a woman who saw a glimmer of a future she'd never dared to imagine before. When they'd been making love, she'd pictured selling up, moving back here, seeing if they could make it work. But she hadn't told him. Of course, she hadn't told him—she'd been pumped with pheromones again, full of him. Afraid he wouldn't feel the same.

Resuming her walk, she tried to force all thoughts of him from her head. What good would it do to indulge in any more of these arbitrary outbreaks of madness? There was a child involved. She'd done the right thing.

Right?

Jero insisted on flying in on every breeze though, the sound of his voice, the feel of his lips on parts of her body that still burned for him. His passion in the bedroom was merely an extension of the way he conducted himself daily—but she'd never had a lover quite like that before. One who just seemed to fit so effortlessly. The first few times with Simon had taken some getting used to. She'd been left thinking 'that was nice' more times than she'd ever thought 'wow, that took me to another dimension!' In fact, the

same could be said for most of her previous sexual encounters. She'd almost come to believe
sex was overrated. Now she knew differently.

Just thinking about the positions they'd tried
made her hot. Stopping under a shady tree, she
answered her ringing phone, and observed two
more kids playing on the shore, where they'd
done the rubbish clean-up on the beach. That
felt like ages ago already. And she was noticing
children everywhere, which was weird. She'd
barely registered them before.

'Hey, stranger!' Mike's voice sounded strange
out of context already. 'Any news on the flight
home?'

She sighed. 'Not yet.'

'Aren't there other flights you could catch?'

Ivy closed her eyes. 'Yes, but those would cost
extra,' she explained. 'I don't have to pay more
if I wait for the same airline.'

'The same airline with faulty engines? That
makes sense, I suppose.'

Her mouth twitched at his Irish dryness.
'What's new from the Blue Stream Veterinary
Alliance, Mike? I haven't checked my email
today.'

'I noticed you'd been taking some time out
from that,' he said. 'That's a good thing, Ivy. But
yeah, they've given us a deadline for an answer.
Six weeks from now. You were supposed to be

back by now, so I guess I'll just tell you while we're here. I kind of want to sell.'

Ivy sucked in a breath. She'd known it in her gut, had felt it coming like an alarm bell on a ticking clock, she'd just been blocking it out.

The parents were cuddling now, watching their happy offspring frolic in neon swimsuits. Her swimming brain took her back to Jero's lovely house the other night, reading Aayla a story, one either side of her bed with its ridiculous *My Little Penguin* bedsheets. They'd matched Aayla's T-shirt. So cute.

In fact, it had felt so warm and loving and cosy in that family unit…like something she'd been missing.

Of course, it had all just freaked her out and she'd left as soon as she could. Stupid really, getting ideas from a man who lived a zillion miles away from her normal life. It wasn't as if the lonely hole she'd spent her childhood in had been filled with anything else, just because she'd met a hot single dad and his kid.

So they'd invited her in—up to a point. Made her feel like part of a family for the first time since her dad died and her mother forgot her existence. They'd also made her forget she had some very adult decisions to make regarding her own baby—her clinic!

'Are you even listening?' Mike seemed to

have realised he was talking about the private equity group's aspirations, and Miss O'Reilly's moulting parakeet, to dead ears, and she continued on along the beach, fanning out her shirt, apologising as her mind reeled with all this information.

'You just don't *want* to come home yet, do you?' he said now, making her pause in her tracks. 'You want to see more of this Jero guy. *And* his daughter.'

'Don't be ridiculous,' she snapped back, making an iguana turn its head to her.

'Well, at least you've switched off for once,' he said. 'There's more to life than work. But you do know, Ivy, your life will only rise to the level you settle for.'

Ivy was struck dumb a second. 'Wow, Mike, Oprah did good.'

'It's not Oprah, but she would probably say that if you weren't still so caught up in the past, maybe you would start to see a different future. For this place, for yourself! Listen, no one could blame you for keeping your heart all bolted up, but sometimes you need to let it out of that steel cage you keep it in...just for a little bit?'

Ivy gaped at the ocean, then bit down on her cheeks. Mike didn't know *all* the details. She'd already opened the door to that steel cage twice...well, she'd opened a bit more than a door, if she was honest. And how bed-shakingly brilliant that had been! But she'd be gone from here in a matter of days, back to Galway, where this would all be past tense and her heart would most certainly protest getting back in its cage. She'd never see them again, and she'd have to try and forget them.

She told Mike as much, noticing how the sound of her words made her feel more and more as if she was lying, denying herself what she really wanted. Mike scoffed at her and reminded her how she'd asked him to mail her old camera to the clinic on Santa Cruz, so Aayla could have it. Jero had refused to let her have her newest one, after all, and she'd wanted to leave the sweet girl with *something* to nurture her talent.

'You're single, Ivy, just enjoy yourself! I'll tell these guys they'll just have to wait a little longer. It's decided,' Mike said. 'Remember, just because I want to sell, you don't have to. Or you could work under new management for a whopping huge salary... There's a lot to think about. You could even work on contract and take extended holidays. Anywhere you wanted to.'

He emphasised *anywhere*. Like he actually meant here, in the Galapagos.

Then he told her he had to go. The parakeet needed him.

'Ivy?' Dudders' voice behind her made her

spin around, just as she'd hung up on Mike. He was carrying a bag of tiny fish she knew were for the kittens and other creatures in the backroom at the clinic. 'I thought that was you. How's the fourth floor of Pelican Hill treating you?'

'Great, thanks,' she managed as her eyes found an unfortunate hole in the crotch of his well-worn elephant pants. 'How's the Darwin Clinic?'

Dudders dutifully recounted the latest happenings. Then he mentioned there was some kind of bug in the new digital system that they couldn't quite figure out how to fix. He looked at her expectantly over his bag of fish. 'Jero said you wanted to enjoy the rest of your time here away from the clinic, which we totally get. *Totally*. But…if you could find a few minutes…'

Ivy moved her camera to the other shoulder, and felt her face contort into a deep scowl as his words sank in. What was happening today? The universe was testing her for sure. First Mike's announcement, now this. Jero had told the other volunteers she had volunteered *not* to be there. How dared he? She'd done nothing of the sort. He was putting words into her mouth.

Her blood started boiling slowly as her mind churned. Yes, she had ended things, but he didn't have to act as if she was already gone, especially if she was *needed*. He'd told her he had no regrets. He'd been lying. He regretted it so much he was actively trying not to involve her in *anything*.

Before she could project her irritation at Jero onto poor Dudders she took another deep breath. 'I have a few minutes,' she told him. Then she forged ahead of him on a beeline for the clinic.

'Ivy!' Aayla squealed and ran from her nanny, Nina, and almost ploughed Ivy over the second she walked in with Dudders. 'I thought you were gone!'

'I was but…' Ivy scanned Reception for Jero while her heart leapt and danced. She hadn't expected Aayla to be here during school hours. As far as she could see, Jero wasn't in the building. She didn't know whether to be disappointed or relieved, but all anger dissipated on the spot. What was she supposed to tell Aayla? They'd already said their goodbyes three days ago.

'I have a sore throat,' Aayla said now, putting her hands around her own neck and pulling a face. She was the picture of adorable in a scarlet headband, a red shirt and jean shorts, with her long brown hair flowing about her face in tendrils. But she did look paler than usual.

'Oh, I'm sorry you're sick, honey,' she found

herself saying, getting to her knees to look her in the eyes. 'When did you start to feel poorly?'

'In maths class.'

Ivy smiled and pushed a lock of hair gently behind the girl's ear. 'Maths used to make me feel the same way.'

'I brought her home from school early,' Nina explained.

'I'm so happy you're here!' Aayla threw her arms around Ivy's shoulders, just as Pluma fluttered out from under the small table by the door. She flew up to perch on a shelf, right on top of the Manila files Ivy had hoped to make redundant, and bobbed her white head towards her. Was she actually saying hello?

Ivy was stunned into silence by both Aayla's embrace, and Pluma's reaction. The bird was getting bigger, and tamer every day. She was roughly the size of a giant crow already, and while she was flying freely wherever she wanted, that still happened to orbit Aayla. Incredible!

'So…the computer…' Dudders had dropped the bag of fish on the desk and was looking at her expectantly again.

'Oh, yes, of course.' Remembering why she'd come, she hurried over and took a seat, placing her camera carefully on the desk.

Ivy was just fixing the issue in the system

when Jero walked through the door. Her heart pole-vaulted to her throat in his presence. His shoulders were hunched, his handsome face was etched in concern. He was wearing the Texas hat again, flip-flops and a navy-blue T-shirt with *STAR Divers* on the back. Drop-dead gorgeous in that casually oblivious way. *Curses.*

He didn't notice her at first. He went straight to Aayla and got to his knees by the little table, where she'd resumed her reading with Nina. *What to do?* Ivy decided it would be a little silly to try and hide behind the laptop and the desk, so she stood and held up her hand. 'Hi, Jero.'

He turned to her in surprise. 'Ivy.'

She tried not to look affected by the mini clowns doing somersaults in her belly. 'I was just getting your files back up and running. If you'd told me sooner you'd have saved a few days' work. Some of what you entered will have to be added again.'

He shrugged, but he did look kind of sheepish as he glanced at the others and cleared his throat. 'I um… I didn't want to bother you.'

More like, you didn't want me here in case I let on how you screwed a tourist's brains out—twice—and then conveniently forgot she existed, she retorted in her head, but she kept her cool. 'It was a small issue with the server. If it happens again, you can just…'

She squared her shoulders and stiffened her spine, realising that whatever she said, if he cared at all, was probably going right over his head. 'I'll write it all down this time if you want.'

Jero didn't speak. He was still staring at her as if she were some feral cat he didn't know what to do with. Was he angry she'd just shown up here? Angry that Aayla knew she was still here, and had just been keeping away from her, for whatever reason? Ugh. Either way, this was awkward. She shouldn't have come.

'Second thoughts, I just remembered, I have to be somewhere.' She snapped the lid down on the laptop. Better to depart with her dignity still intact.

'Ivy, wait.' Jero made to step towards her, one hand outstretched, but in a second Pluma flew from the shelf and dived between them, making a grab for the bag of fish that Dudders had left on the desk. The determined bird swiped it up with her beak but in a flash the bag split at the seams. Tiny fish rained like stinky hailstones over the entire reception area, and, to her horror, all over their heads.

Nina gasped. Jero swiped at his arms and neck. Pluma started gobbling something up from the top of a pile of books. Mortified, Ivy just stood there, watching something small and silver slither lifelessly from her hand to the floor.

Oh, my God!

It felt as if time froze. Then, out of nowhere, Aayla burst out laughing, clutching her stomach, her sore throat apparently forgotten. In seconds, Nina followed, chortling behind her hand. To her shock and somewhat relief, Jero started laughing too. Just the sound of them all flicked a switch in her, till she was laughing so hard she could barely stand up straight, observing the pool of fish now covering the floor. That bird...

'See!' Aayla cried. 'Pluma just doesn't want you to go, Ivy!'

Ivy shook her head and swiped a hand across her forehead. Jero caught her eye, and she felt her cheeks flame. Maybe the kid was right— who knew how smart boobies were, really? At least being showered in fish had eased the tension between her and Jero. Not that she wasn't still annoyed at him for telling everyone she didn't *want* to be here. That would have to be addressed.

The door behind them swung open. 'Help me, please!'

The laughter stopped abruptly. Ivy followed Jero's eyes to the tear-stained teenager who'd just staggered inside, crying her eyes out. In her arms was something limp that looked far too big and heavy for her to be holding.

CHAPTER THIRTEEN

JERO WAS STILL processing Aayla's sore throat, the shower of fish in Reception and Ivy's sudden re-appearance, and now the teen was talking a million miles an hour. Summoning calm, he threw the house keys to Nina and motioned to her to take Aayla home. Ivy was already ushering the girl and the dog she was carrying through to the back.

He met her in the OR, where she tossed him scrubs and gloves and set about injecting the dog while the teen stood watching them with watery eyes. 'You don't have to stay,' he whispered in Ivy's ear, catching her arm.

He'd been about to tell her thanks for the new system, before the fish incident. He hadn't wanted it implemented one little bit, but it had certainly made things a lot easier round here… before it broke down. But she was here again when she should be out there enjoying the island.

'Is that another way of saying you don't *want*

me to stay?' she retorted in a hiss, eyes narrowed over the needle she was holding. 'You told everyone here I didn't want to work here any more. We didn't exactly agree on that part, Jero.'

Damn.

He didn't have time to respond before she'd turned to Dudders. 'Dudders, Jero and I have got this. Take this lady out front, please.'

Jero watched Dudders lead the teen towards the door. His volunteers had come to trust and rely on Ivy almost as much as him, and he'd gone and told her to stay away. He watched her with a frown. He'd had his reasons for that at the time and allowing her time alone to see the island was the least selfish one of them. He didn't trust himself around her.

But here she was, and he did need her. The dog had been run over. It looked like a dachshund/beagle mix, no more than ten months old.

'Degloving to the left paw,' Ivy observed over the table as they inspected the male dog's toenails. They were all but peeling off with his skin and fur—a proper mess. Thankfully Aayla had been too distracted by Pluma and the fish back there to register all this.

'Can you save him?' The teary teen was still hovering in the doorway, looking between them hopefully from beside another cage of mewing kittens that wouldn't have fitted in the storeroom with the others. 'I brought him straight here.'

'He'll be OK,' Jero assured her, meeting Ivy's eyes again and trying not to register the agitation that still lingered in the depth of her stare. This was not the time to be thinking about how they'd left things…or how he'd been practically sitting on his hands every night since, to stop himself sprinting to her apartment to continue where they'd left off.

'The dog…the poor thing…he just stood there and let the scooter hit him…' The teen refused to move her eyes away, even as Dudders continued urging her away.

'We'll take care of him,' Ivy cut in, before he could.

It seemed as if the driver had sped off without even looking back, which happened a lot. Most of their injured animals came in having been struck by cars or scooters. The poor girl had been right behind the offending scooter on her own bike and seen the hit and run.

'Please, do what you can! I think he was injured even before this happened,' she told them from the doorway, right before Dudders finally managed to coax her out to Reception, swiping a mop and bucket on the way past, to clear up the fish no doubt.

The X-rays didn't look good. 'She's right.

He was likely born with a deformed wrist,' Ivy said, studying them alongside him some minutes later. 'I think it was fused in a bent position…it was probably his deformity that led to this paw injury. He just wasn't quick enough to pull the limb out of the way and stop himself from getting run over. Poor little man.'

'I think we have to amputate,' Jero said solemnly.

Ivy's eyes narrowed over the sedated dog. 'Once it's gone, he'll adapt quite quickly on three legs, I'm sure. But right now, he's in too much pain to go on enjoying life.'

'That makes two of us,' he followed.

'What?' Ivy crossed her arms. 'Are you comparing yourself to a dog, Jero?'

A stupid lovesick puppy maybe, he thought, annoyed with himself.

'Let's get on with it, then,' he muttered, wishing his mind and heart would agree on how they felt about Ivy.

Together they attended to their casualty in silence, but he felt it like electricity every time their arms or fingers brushed. He'd missed her presence around here; missed walking in and seeing her fiery curls and pearly smile and the way she was around Aayla, which had left an impression on the kid, he couldn't deny. Aayla wanted to be a wildlife photographer now, amongst other things.

What a woman, messing with his head like this. He frowned to himself, trying to focus on the stitches. Helping the wounded animal was paramount but seeing her again so unexpectedly had mowed him over like the dog. The last few days without her, he'd thought about her constantly, like an itch he couldn't scratch. Aayla hadn't let it go: *'Ivy this... Ivy that... Daddy, Pluma misses Ivy!'*

'Why did you tell everyone I didn't want to be here?' she asked him now, snapping off her gloves. Jero lowered the sleeping, three-legged dog into a crate beside the mewing kittens and felt her eyes on his back. He cleared his throat.

'I was testing myself, I guess, to see what it would be like when you were really gone. It was very quiet.' It was the truth, wasn't it?

'You are *still* going, Ivy,' he added as the familiar tightening started up around his throat.

'You're right. I have a life to get back to,' she said behind him. 'I should be there already really...especially as Mike wants to sell his half of the business. He just told me. Just now. It won't be the same without him. I can either sell out and leave myself or stay on under new management...my gosh.' She made a harangued sound. 'I'm thinking out loud again. I don't know why I'm even telling you this.'

Ivy went quiet, and he tried to ignore the thudding of his heart. He knew a cry for help when he heard one; despite everything, she wanted his input, or advice. He didn't *want* to care what she did next—it was definitely best if he didn't…

He settled the dog on the blankets, took his time locking the cage and heard her removing the coat she'd pulled on, button by button. Once she'd hung that back on the wall, she'd be gone again. Back to her complicated life, which would in no way involve him and Aayla from all the way over in Ireland, whatever she decided to do.

'It all happened so fast, with us.' She sighed, behind him. 'I took offence that you didn't want to see me here, but you're right, it would have been complicated if I'd carried on working with you—this is awkward enough! Me talking about my life like you should even care…'

'Ivy, of course I care.'

She held up her hand as he turned to her. 'It's fine, Jero. We had our fun. I know you're busy, probably thinking about this trial and everything else, and I know you have to think about Aayla and who influences her in what ways, especially after what your ex-wife did—'

'This has nothing to do with Suranne,' he cut in.

Ivy's eyes grew wide. He cursed himself for his defensive tone. He shouldn't have said it like that. He wanted to believe Ivy had been a temporary distraction, a bit of fun, but it had evolved into far more. How was it that he cared so damn much about her with every passing second? That was why he was mad, he realised. He might have developed feelings for Ivy faster than he had for Suranne. Would he ever learn?

'I have to go check on Aayla,' he said gruffly, removing his coat and tossing it onto the laundry basket. 'I have to shower this damn fish smell off me. I'll hand this over to Dudders on the way out.'

She blinked at him, tossed her own coat on top of his with a strength that defied her size, then crossed her arms again, lips pursed. Flames ignited in her amber eyes. He took a step towards her, then stopped just short of her shoes.

'Thank you for your help today,' he said, willing himself not to cross a line, and not to be affected by the perfect storm of hurt and fury on her face. 'And congratulations on having grown such a great business that someone else would like to buy it.' He gestured around them, just as a poster peeled from the wall again. 'That's not an easy accomplishment for anyone but you did it. It must be something incredible, waiting for you back in Galway.'

'What you do *here* is incredible, Jero,' she responded, stepping away to stick the poster up again with a firm slap of her palm. 'If you can't see how much I really mean that, how much you inspire me, how much you make me think I should just…'

She caught herself and huffed at the floor.

He stared at her, thrown. 'You should just what? What were you going to say?'

'It doesn't matter,' she mumbled, which implied it mattered very much but she'd decided not to say it anyway. Then she swept out of the room in a breeze of wet fish, which somehow still left him wanting her even more.

Jero was reading the latest notes on the illegal trawler case when the doorbell rang. He tutted under his breath. It was after nine p.m. and Aayla was sleeping upstairs. Her throat was still sore. He didn't need her waking up. Expecting one of the neighbours, he flung the door open, then did a double take.

'Ivy.'

'I left my camera at the clinic, and I don't have keys,' she said, too coldly for his liking. He told her he'd brought it here after she'd stormed out earlier. He would have delivered it to her himself tomorrow. Maybe.

'I didn't think you'd want to see me,' he added,

pointing her through to the kitchen, where the camera sat on the dining table.

She picked it up, looking around the kitchen warily, and he regretted not doing the dishes. 'Thanks for keeping it safe.' She sighed, clutching it to her chest. He shoved his hands in his pockets. She smelled like flowers and shower cream now and looked sexy as hell in a long flowing dress the colour of ocean shallows.

'I owe you an apology,' he said. 'Want to sit?'

Her lips compressed, sending the flesh around them white. The two remaining puppies scampered around her while he swept a pile of papers and stray clean napkins and Aayla's toy cars to the end of the table.

'You were right, what you said earlier. What happened with my ex changed everything for Aayla, and me... I shouldn't have snapped. I just don't like being reminded of all the ways I've screwed things up for Aayla.'

Ivy frowned down her nose at him as he dropped to one of the wooden chairs. 'What are you even talking about?'

'Well, I failed at providing the one thing a growing girl needs most, for a start—her mother,' he said, wheeling a toy digger towards him and back again with one finger. 'It's a sore point.'

Ivy dropped to the chair beside his and put a hand to his arm, stopping the digger in its tracks.

'The fact that your ex chose another life away from here isn't *your fault*, Jero,' she said on a sigh. 'Island life is tough. It's no reflection on you. Aayla worships you! So does everyone else I've met around this place. You've built a family around you right here. And if you must know...it's one of the nicest things I've ever felt a part of.'

She fixed her eyes on the puppies a second, who were trying to jump onto another chair. 'I never had a mother around me either, remember. But I'm OK. You're enough, Jero, don't tell yourself anything else.'

He felt a smile flicker across his lips. So, she wasn't mad at him any more. This was good—he'd been kicking himself all night for the way they'd left things. As usual he'd stopped himself going to her when he'd wanted to.

'Thank you,' he said. Her lips were so tempting as usual, but he couldn't kiss her. He wouldn't kiss her.

'OK, so your tech and organisational skills have their limitations,' she followed. 'And you would be murdered for wearing flip-flops in *my* clinic...but those are minor issues.'

He smiled broadly as Ivy dodged his play thump. He couldn't kiss her, but he didn't want this to end either. 'I like when you sing my praises,' he said.

'Don't get used to it.'

'You never really talked about *your* mother much,' he tested. 'Or your father.'

Ivy scooped up a puppy, cradling it to her chest. Then she asked for a glass of wine.

Without pause he crossed to the fridge and grabbed a bottle.

Two glasses later, and she'd told him everything.

Ivy had been too young at four and a half years old to understand the meaning of death. She'd only known that a new kind of emptiness and darkness had settled into the house in her father's place. Ivy's dog Zeus had lain on the doormat for a week with his big head on his paws, waiting. She'd sat with him, telling him it would be OK. Knowing deep down it wouldn't.

She told him how Etta Malone—former mother of the year—launched herself like an Irishwoman-sized missile into her work after that. She sounded like a force to be reckoned with. The first female CEO in her sector who'd bulleted through the gender gap in the tech industry, teaching women how to code. A real role model, so everyone said. Late nights, early morning starts… Ivy had barely seen her for the best part of a decade.

'Mum just made work her everything. Like she could possibly outrun her grief if she distracted herself enough. I guess it took me a while to realise that she was grieving the whole time. She probably thought she was helping me in some way, not exposing me to her misery. But kids know things. They know more than we think.'

'Tell me about it,' he said, offering to top up her wine as he led her to the living area. He moved his guitar from the couch, but she sat at the other end from him and crossed her legs under her, eyes fixed on *The Hungry Caterpillar* on the coffee table.

'I could hear her crying in her bed at midnight, she missed him so much. If I ever tried to go in there, she'd shoo me away. I guess I felt shut out, you know? But I didn't want her to feel worse by bringing it up. So we went on like that, quietly existing on two opposite sides of a wall. I don't know who was more closed-off in the end. Me, or her.'

'Are you still in touch now?' he asked, forcing himself not to stretch his legs out, where they might touch her in any way. Should she even be here? Probably not. If Aayla woke up she'd find Ivy here, and Aayla was already starting to look at Ivy as if she was the greatest thing since Lego.

Ivy sipped her wine, and he wondered if she

usually talked about all this stuff. 'She paid for this honeymoon. She wasn't a bad mother; she just didn't exactly give me confidence that you can juggle a family with a career. Things weren't exactly perfect with Simon, but the catalyst to the break-up was the fact that I didn't want a family, not with how hard I work... I'm probably just as busy as my own mother was.'

'But you don't have to be that busy, do you?'

Ivy squeezed her eyes shut and shook her head in her palm quickly. 'I can't believe I'm telling you all this.'

He studied her flushed cheeks. Was she changing her mind, after getting to know Aayla? He might be biased but Aayla was a pretty great advocate for spending time with kids. 'You can juggle anything, I've watched you,' he told her, feeling the oddest sense of pride sweep through him for how she'd overcome such adversity, started out on her own and achieved so much already. She herself was a force to be reckoned with. He leaned forwards, his hand finding her knee over her dress.

'I think you'd be a great mother—just look at how much Aayla loves you already.'

The second he said it, he retracted. 'Not that I'm looking for a replacement mother for Aayla.' His wine glass clattered against the coffee table as he put it down. 'I mean...'

'And I'm not looking to be anyone's replacement mother,' she confirmed at lightning speed. Her fingers were white around the stem of her glass. He thought it might actually break. A jolt ricocheted around his heart.

What the hell had made him say that?

'Maybe we shouldn't have had this wine.' Ivy placed her glass down and stood up, but he caught her elbow. This time she landed right beside him, and a small helpless moan escaped her lips. 'I get it, Ivy. You don't *want* a kid. I get it, but what did you just say to me? You're enough.'

'I know that.' She leaned into his palm as he cradled her face, then placed her hand over his, against her cheek. She might know that, but it still looked as if she was fighting some kind of silent battle in her head.

He emphasised it again. 'You're more than enough. But when you go home…back to your business that apparently someone wants to buy for big money, promise me you'll think about what you really want, and what really matters to you,' he said. 'I'd hate to think of you missing out on anything.'

She scanned his eyes, searching, that look of confusion still creasing her brow. Her voice was choked when she spoke. 'Why do you care so much?'

He traced a finger over her lips, memorising

the shape of them with his flesh. Mixed feelings assailed him as Ivy caught his other hand. 'You're special,' he told her, against his own will. His mind, mouth and body were simply not aligning on how they should act around this woman any more.

'Stop making me *not* want to go home, Jero,' she said, lowering her head. He tilted her chin up.

'Well, stop making me want to ask you to stay.'

Rational thoughts became impossible. He couldn't tell who kissed who first but in seconds they were a tangle of limbs on the couch, and he was being forced to remember how addictive her intense sensuality was as she blazed a trail of kisses from his lips across his throat, hoisting up his shirt at the same time, straddling him, locking him down with her thighs.

Ferocious kisses grew softer, guided by their hearts more than their hands for once. He really was in deep. Already. He was going to be ruined when she was gone, and he was probably walking into disaster with every passing second, but what was he supposed to do?

He couldn't keep away.

He led her upstairs to the bedroom, tiptoeing past Aayla's door, and a hunger, deeper and stronger than anything sexual, rumbled in his bloodstream and did its best to consume him.

Pressing into her on the bed, he wanted nothing more than to satisfy Ivy and share in her pleasures and pain; to know every inch of her, every cell and story.

He'd never known desire and longing like this for anyone, never dared to imagine anything so intense after…after everything he'd suffered through to get here. Why not just give in and let himself enjoy her, while she was still here?

CHAPTER FOURTEEN

Two weeks later, Ivy stared at the email, feeling her stomach sink. The flight home had left twelve days ago without her, and unless she took the next one, leaving three days from now, she'd lose her free seat. So far, she'd procrastinated and made excuses, spending her days and nights blocking out reality in a blissful bubble of hot sex with Jero.

It was more than hot sex, actually. She loved being at their dining table most, listening to them talk over homework. She loved cooking with Aayla and laughing at Pluma, and telling them both about Ireland, watching the looks on their faces, as if it were some strange, distant land she'd invented. Sometimes, her real life felt like a dream even to herself.

But their conversation that night, when she'd come to collect her camera, hadn't left her head. So Jero wasn't looking for a replacement mother for Aayla, which was totally understandable.

She didn't want to be one and she'd told him as much. Maybe a little too quickly, in retrospect.

But the jolt to her heart when he'd first said that, and again, when he'd outright stated how obvious it was that she didn't want a child herself, it still stung. It made her feel less than what he needed...which should have been fine. She had a life to get back to after all.

But it was also confusing as hell.

Kids. Ugh. She'd never wanted that in her life before, not at all, but the reasons for that felt at odds with her heart now, the more time she spent around Aayla. Of course, Aayla was great. Maybe it was just *her* she enjoyed; rather than the notion of herself as a mother.

What was this feeling?

It was taking some processing, for sure.

Thanks to a virtual campaign and a new set of posters around town, designed by Aayla herself, they had managed to rehome the last of the puppies together. And several litters of kittens. Projects like this were starting to feel suspiciously like fun, even though they ate into her email time. But while time had considerably slowed since she'd let herself enjoy each moment away from *work*, it had never stopped ticking.

She should really just stop procrastinating and book the flight!

'Ivy, where should I put Tripod? We need the cage for the new puppies.'

Ivy pulled her fingers from the laptop keys. Zenon was looking around him in confusion for a place to put their three-legged dog. He'd just had his final check-up after the amputation two weeks ago, and she felt herself getting rattled again. Zenon had come in late—again—and had missed the stand-up, where she'd already informed the team of volunteers, including a new girl from Australia, of the schedule.

'The girl who brought him in is collecting him within the hour—she adopted him, remember? Just take him for a walk. Then you can clean the cage for the pups.'

He gave her a salute and made to leave for the back room. *Second thoughts.*

She called out after him. 'He's not called Tripod, she called him Alpha. And you know what, Zenon, there are lots of people who'd like to be on the volunteering schedule. If you don't have time for it any more, all you need to do is tell me... Jero. Tell Jero.'

Zenon's shoulders sagged. To her shock he went bright red from his florally tattooed legs up to his cheeks and stammered an apology. He promised to do better, told her how much he respected her for bringing it up. Jero had tried to pull him up on it several times apparently, before giving up and simply delegating more responsibilities to Dudders and herself instead, but it wasn't good enough and she told him so. Not on her watch.

She tried not to let the tension get to her as she continued with her consultations. A flea treatment, an ingrown claw…it all merged into one as her mind mulled over her situation. She *was* leaving. She had to book this flight. Mike wanted to sell, and so did she.

Maybe.

She still couldn't decide. Every day meant a different emotion around that, too. She'd kept it quiet so far, because the thought of giving up her baby—her clinic—was drastic and terrifying, but maybe it *was* time for something else. The thought wouldn't budge; that maybe she *could* spend more time here, sell up and invest in the Darwin Clinic, if Jero would even allow it? There was so much to be done.

It felt too abstract and strange to consider saying out loud. At night, it kept her awake. She'd taken to studying the exquisite lines and angles of Jero's sleeping face on the pillow beside hers, wondering what the hell was happening to her. Simon kept flashing into her mind, too. Simon had never given her these feelings. He'd never given her the sense that, with him at her side, she could make a difference to the world.

Simon was a good man, but he had never left her flailing in the wind, wondering where she stood or what she'd do without him. In fact, she had always been in control. She hadn't wanted kids, and that had been fine with him—till it wasn't. That was why she'd felt so safe with him, for so long.

Safe, yes, but ultimately unsatisfied...

Jero had encouraged her, that night they'd made love for the first time in his bed. He'd got her thinking more and more about what she wanted. That night, he'd let her in, let down his walls, and she'd let herself consider that this might be something real, something worth holding onto, against all odds.

But that was crazy, wasn't it? Intense emotional flings didn't last for ever; they were called flings for a reason! Besides, he hadn't said anything definitive at all along the lines of, 'Stay with me!'

So what if she thought he felt it every time they made love? Even if he did, he was right to be concerned, and work towards an official goodbye. Despite what he'd said about her potentially being a great mother in the future—or the fact that it somehow meant more than when Simon had said it—she was already thinking about new projects to get involved in, filling up her days as she always did. What kind of role model would she be in the long run? He must know that. She was no good for them.

Just book the flight, Ivy!

'Ivy, where's the extension lead?' Dudders asked now. 'I need to plug this new heat lamp in for the lizard.'

He waved a lamp in front of her, and she admitted defeat, and shut the laptop. 'There's an extension lead in the closet over there, I think,' she said. 'I don't know how old it is. You should ask Jero when he gets back.'

'I'm sure it's fine,' Dudders said cheerily. 'Oh, can you help me shift some of the other plugs around?'

Ivy sighed. She'd book the flight later. And it was time to tell Jero she was leaving for good.

That afternoon, Aayla met her with Nina and Pluma following close by, at the community talk Jero was hosting on the beach. Dee, their friendly conservationist from the tortoise sanctuary, waved at her, as did Angie, the lady who'd come to Jero's house to choose a puppy.

It was late afternoon and the sun cast long, spindly shadows across the sand. The light made all the people who'd flocked to hear him look extra shiny and golden. In moments like this, Ivy couldn't help imagining how rainy it would be when she landed back in Ireland.

Aayla led her by the hand to the chair she'd been saving for her, right at the front.

'Daddy's going to talk,' she announced, and Ivy's heart did a silly schoolgirl skip the second he stepped onto the makeshift stage.

He retrieved a kitten from an oversized pocket in his army shorts, and the kids all rushed to the front, kneeling before the stage to get the chance to hold it, while he relayed the importance of the mobile clinic.

'Don't be afraid to bring your cats and dogs to one of our mobile stations. The more we protect against unwanted domestic animals, the safer our islands will be against diseases…'

He was halfway through his speech, and Ivy was growing sicker, wondering where and how she'd tell him she was finally leaving, when Marsha, the friendly fishmonger from the market, made an appearance. She looked frazzled to say the least. Ivy crept past Aayla and Nina. Something wasn't right.

'Sorry, I know you're busy…but it's Álvaro.' Marsha scraped a hand through her greying hair. Perspiration glistened on her forehead, as if she'd run or cycled here at lightning speed, afraid for the sea lion.

'What's wrong with Álvaro?'

Marsha explained how he hadn't been at the market in two days, which was most unlike him.

Someone had just informed her of an injured sea lion that matched his description. 'He's on the beach around the bay. You can't get there without a boat. The guys who found him couldn't bring him in. He was scared, and violent. I need you to take me to him.'

'Me?' Ivy was stunned.

'You and Jero. He knows Jero. He knows all of us, maybe he'll let us help him?'

Some people in the audience had turned in their seats and were watching her and Marsha, instead of Jero. Jero noticed. With a frown he excused himself from the stage. In minutes he'd been given some keys to a boat and was calling Dudders to meet them at the harbour with emergency medical supplies.

It wasn't Dudders waiting at the harbour with the supplies. It was Zenon.

'What are you doing here?' Jero looked suspicious as he tossed the bag into the boat. He'd sent Nina home with Aayla, even after Aayla begged to join them. Secretly Ivy was impressed with Zenon. He wasn't usually available on call, especially this late. He was usually out on a date with a tourist or sleeping.

'Just wanted to do my bit,' Zenon said, throwing a secret smile her way. 'I hope our old boy Álvaro is OK. And hey, Jero, I just wanted to apologise if I've seemed a little unenthusiastic about being here. I'm going to change.'

Jero looked as if Zenon had tasered him for a moment, but he slapped his back good-naturedly and told him it was all good. Ivy nodded her thanks in Zenon's direction as their boat sped away. Good. He'd really listened to her.

The wind tussled with her hair as they cruised around the coast with Pluma soaring on the wind along with them. Never one to miss out on anything exciting, the bird had left Aayla, maybe sensing she was safe, and flown with the grown-ups instead?

Jero caught her eye and she felt her stomach clench, knowing she had to tell him she was leaving. How would he react? He knew she was going eventually, of course, even if they hadn't talked about it yet. Maybe she'd been stalling, falling in love a bit more every day... *Setting yourself up for a real fall,* she added in her head.

'Are you OK over there?' Jero's question was directed at her, and Ivy looked to the water passing by in a blur.

Thankfully Marsha answered for her. 'I'm OK, just thinking about poor Álvaro.'

'Me too,' Ivy said quickly. Darn the stupid tears in her eyes. Yes, she was thinking about Álvaro too but the thought of getting on that plane or upsetting Aayla was setting her off again. Her brain felt bruised to a livid purple welt. She should just say it now; tell them both she was booking her flight, jetting out of here in three days.

Why couldn't she do it?

'Álvaro? Oh, my poor old friend!' Marsha was the first to leap from the boat to the shore when Jero pulled into the shallows.

Ivy felt his hand on the small of her back as they crossed the sand towards the giant sea lion. 'He doesn't look happy,' she said despondently, the second they got close enough. Jero's brow furrowed in concern. Fishing netting was everywhere, burrowed hard into Álvaro's fins, where he'd failed to wriggle out of it. The tangle of blue and green mesh and blood tore at her heart.

Jero looked angry and searched for a knife in the supply bag. 'It could be extras from that trawler.' Then he held her back from getting any closer. The poor thing was bellowing in agony.

'We need to get this off you.' Marsha was visibly upset as she made to tug at the fishing nets. Álvaro snorted and huffed, but to Ivy's relief he didn't make a lunge for her. It was quite remarkable, Ivy thought, how trusting some of these animals were with humans. Especially humans they were used to.

'I can't stand all this blood on him!' Marsha

was getting teary, and Jero stopped her tugging at the nets again. There was so much netting, it was a wonder the creature could still move. Ivy copied Jero, holding up her hands, shushing and soothing him. Marsha stroked his big silky face gently, all the while whispering that they were trying to help him.

'Maybe he's OK…' Ivy started.

Suddenly, Álvaro turned to them with a deafening honk and reared up like a circus performer. He roared in fright, making her gasp. A scream chilled Ivy's blood. Then she realised it was her own.

'Ivy, get back!' Jero yanked her backwards into him before the sea lion could land on top of her. Breathless, she froze in his arms, before he ushered her away, and urged her to sit down on the sand. She was shaking. He crouched in front of her. 'He would have crushed every bone in your body,' he stated, one hand on her knee. 'You scared the emojis out of me!'

She sucked in a breath as he put a hand to her cheek and brushed her curls aside, in full view of Marsha. He hadn't touched her in front of anyone before and she didn't miss the look of surprise on Marsha's face. Her heart started thrumming even faster.

'What's she doing?' Marsha's attention was on Pluma now. Pluma had flown to the sea lion's head and was making soft, soothing clucking sounds. Bird language for 'calm down'?

Strangely it seemed to work wonders. They watched a moment while Ivy tried to calm herself down at the same time. Eventually, she let Jero help her up to her feet, and Álvaro remained completely still while they set about cutting the remaining netting from his fins with knives.

'He's not as badly hurt as it looks,' Jero assured Marsha. 'Sea lions have very tough skin; they need it to live on land and in the sea, like they do. He'll heal just fine, maybe a few scars.'

'But what about all the blood?'

'It's just blood. Everybody bleeds.'

Marsha nodded, running her gaze between them. 'I guess you both know what you're doing.'

Ivy stayed quiet, wishing she could quell her nerves. Somehow, knowing Marsha was on to them made her anxious. Was she talking about the sea lion, or was she implying Jero might not have thought this through—getting involved with her?

Just then Álvaro swivelled on the sand and slipped loose of the last of the netting they'd been slicing at and waddled into the water. Pluma soared overheard. Marsha started cheering like a football fan in an instant, running behind him the whole way.

'Thank God, he's going to be OK,' Jero whispered, almost under his breath.

He brought her hand to his lips but stopped just short of kissing her when Marsha turned around. He wasn't quick enough. Ivy flushed. What was happening?

'So, you two are…a thing, huh?' Marsha threw Jero a look that told Ivy she was more concerned for him than she'd dare say in front of her. She tensed, waiting for him to say something.

And waited.

And waited.

He said nothing. Jero just shrugged and cleared his throat and kept his eyes on Álvaro.

Shame blasted her from all angles. They weren't a thing; she was a fling. At least that was what he was implying with his silence, right? He was embarrassed to have been caught out, to have slipped up again with a tourist. Maybe she'd been waiting for a declaration of some kind that he would never make.

Ugh. This had gone too far. She was just delaying the misery now. She'd book her flight tonight, she decided.

CHAPTER FIFTEEN

JERO STOPPED HIMSELF from cursing out loud down the phone as Nina's croaky voice apologised profusely. It wasn't Nina's fault she'd come down with gastro, but he was due to leave for Quito tomorrow. The trial was looming and now there was no one to watch Aayla while he was gone.

He stacked a pile of scattered books on the kitchen table, wondering what to do. He could ask Marsha—but Marsha had to be at the market stall at five every morning. Besides, he was a little annoyed at her for sticking her nose into his business the other day, asking if he and Ivy were a thing like that, looking at him as though he might regret it. He'd almost said, *Yes, of course...wasn't it obvious?* But then Ivy had said nothing either and he didn't want to assume anything or turn them into village gossip.

He needed to talk with her privately about where they stood. He couldn't say what he was feeling any more, out of some stupid fear of rejection. Ivy wasn't Suranne, and what they'd built in such a short space of time was special. He'd realised that the second she was almost crushed by a sea lion.

As for now…

Aayla could stay with a friend, he supposed, but he'd rather Aayla stayed at home—no one in their right mind would want Pluma flapping around their house and the two came as a package deal these days. The bird went outside whenever she wanted, but she was still leaving enough feathers around the place to stuff a pillow with.

Not a bad idea for a Christmas gift, he thought idly, just as the doorbell rang.

Ivy stood there looking gorgeous as usual in another green top and jean shorts. 'I wasn't expecting you,' he said as she stepped past him without stopping to accept the kiss he'd been about to drop on her lips.

He hadn't seen her much since the Álvaro episode. She'd been busy. So had he; but he'd missed her. She smiled weakly and held up a bottle of freshly squeezed orange juice.

In the kitchen she eyed his half-packed bag. 'You pack in the kitchen?' She half laughed, collecting two glasses from the cupboard above the sink.

'I was packing the coffee before I forget. Hotel coffee sucks. Then Nina called me. She's sick.'

Ivy walked around the table, sipping her juice. She picked up Aayla's latest drawings of her new obsession, Álvaro, while he explained what had happened.

The rare bird they'd found on the second detained ship had turned out to be the last of its species. Someone as yet unidentified had stolen it from a sanctuary on Floreana. Now, thanks to new supposed 'evidence' and a stream of outrage from environmentalists worldwide, all of which was being broadcast on more television channels than he cared to count, the trial was an even bigger deal than before. He didn't want to go at all, but he was a representative for the island community more than just a witness to the event itself, and he owed it to everyone to help bring these people to justice.

'I might be gone a few days at least, in Quito,' he explained. 'I was kind of counting on Nina to stay here with her.'

'Poor Nina,' Ivy empathised, still looking at the drawings. She seemed paler than usual and tired, he realised, studying her over his OJ. As if she'd been awake all night. When he asked what was up, she told him nothing was wrong.

She was lying.

Was it them she was thinking about? This

'*thing*' they'd somehow fallen into, which now included one of them bringing orange juice to the other in the mornings? Or was she about to tell him she was leaving? The sudden thought was chilling.

'Ivy, we need to talk…'

'Why don't I stay with her, while you're away?' Ivy's eyes were brighter now, searching his.

'Oh, really, you?' He hadn't been expecting that. 'You don't have to do that,' he followed quickly. As if he'd impose like that! She was always so busy, not least with the volunteer duties she was still assigning herself, and the acquisition back home.

'I'm serious, Jero, if you need someone to stay with Aayla, I'd be happy to.'

Oh. OK.

Jero found his hand moving to his mouth. He stroked his chin thoughtfully, staring at the cutlery drawer. Ivy mumbled something under her breath behind him.

'Of course, it's a stupid idea, why would you want me doing that?' she followed, but he was considering it now. If she really *wanted* to…

He trusted her, he realised suddenly. With Aayla. In his home. He couldn't stop thinking how quickly they'd bonded. How reticent he'd been at first to let it happen, but how it had happened anyway. A lot like their own relationship.

He turned. Ivy was looking at him warily. 'Forget I ever mentioned it. There must be someone else more suitable—'

'No, no,' he interjected, crossing to her. 'If you're sure it's what you want to do, I can get the volunteers to cover some of your shifts. Or all of them. You can stay here with her and Pluma.'

'Whatever works,' she said with an insouciant shrug, looking around the room instead of up at him.

'You know, for a second I thought you were going to announce you'd booked your flight home,' he admitted in relief, resting on a corner of the kitchen table.

Ivy flushed red and looked to the floor. He drew her towards him between his legs, worried now that he couldn't read her.

'I know you must be thinking about your practice back home; all the things you have to do in Galway?' His throat felt dry and tight as he said it, but he squeezed her hands, psyching himself up for the right words to leave his mouth.

'You know, Aayla wants to visit you in Ireland? She says she wants to photograph the Giant's Causeway.' He paused, tracing her lips with his eyes. 'I was thinking maybe... I could come with her, to photograph the Giant's Causeway? And maybe you could come back here with us after. See to it that Pluma doesn't miss you too much?'

Ivy's eyes grew wide as saucers. He watched them fill with joy and relief before she wrapped her arms around his shoulders, flooding him with her sensual scent and the kind of hope he hadn't dared feel until right this very moment. 'That's what you needed to talk to me about?'

He stood, then took her face in his hands. 'You're not even gone yet, and I miss you. Maybe we can make something work. I know it's a lot to think about, and nothing needs to happen right away but…'

He trailed off. Ivy looked troubled again now, drumming her nails against her side. He held his breath, searching her face. 'Ivy…did I say the wrong thing?'

She shook her head. 'No, no, not at all,' she said, taking his hands again. 'Of course, I want to think about this…it's just, I thought, after you didn't reply to Marsha's question about us being a thing…'

'Why would I confirm anything to Marsha when we haven't even discussed it ourselves? I've been waiting to talk to you. Things have just been so crazy with this trial and everything else.'

She nodded, smiling slightly. 'I suppose I

didn't say anything either. It's all been such a whirlwind.'

'I'll only be gone a few days,' he said, allowing a sense of relief to wash over him, finally. 'We can talk more when I get back.' He pulled her against him, till her hips dug deliciously into his flesh. 'But right now… I think I should show you a couple of things in the bedroom, you know, just in case you have any problems while I'm away?'

'I think that's the best idea I've heard all day.' She grinned.

CHAPTER SIXTEEN

DAY ONE OF babysitting. Ivy's mother sounded more interested than she'd heard her in years. 'You're still in the Galapagos? What's going on?'

Ivy pressed the phone to her ear and continued stirring the cake mix, while Aayla did her best to pour the first lot of chocolate gloop into the silicone cups they'd laid out. She'd already managed to get more on the counter than in the cups, and her face was covered in chocolate already.

'Who told you?' Ivy asked, wishing every cell of her body didn't tense up every time they talked.

'I bumped into Mike at the shop, he was on his lunch break. He said you were taking some more holiday time. Are you OK? You're not sick, are you?'

Pluma let out a squawk and zoomed from the shelf behind her, clattering onto a pile of dry dishes. Aayla giggled, waving her chocolate-covered spatula about to a made-up song about cake.

'What the blazes is going on?' Her mother had always said *What the blazes?* and Ivy almost laughed.

'Just making cupcakes with Jero's daughter and her booby, and no, I'm not sick, just because I took some more holiday.'

'Her what?'

Ivy dutifully explained the bird situation as best she could in the midst of the total chaos erupting around her.

'So let me get this straight. Instead of working out the details of a multimillion-euro acquisition with your business partner and equity firm, you're adopting wildlife and baking cupcakes... Ivy, I don't know what to say. Are you sure you're not sick?'

She let her mother berate her decisions as she pushed a stool over to the oven, so Aayla could reach it to turn it on. *That's right, one hundred and eighty degrees,* she mouthed, just as Aayla racked it up to three hundred and Pluma decided to land on the girl's head, making her shriek again and almost fall off the stool.

Ivy caught her, and assured her mother everything was fine, she still had time to talk equity, though Etta Malone was obviously getting worried about her mental health. Which was ironic. It had only been in adulthood, when she'd made a name and career for herself in veterinary medicine, that her mother had shown any interest in what she was doing at all. Although, maybe that was unfair, she mused, considering what her mother had gone through, losing the love of her life.

She'd still put food on the table, she'd still given her a roof and an education, and her animals. She should be grateful her mother stuck around and didn't jet off altogether—as *some* people did.

As for herself, right now she was having a blast, even though time was ticking...*tick-tick-tick*...

'I was about to fly home, Mum,' she said now, sliding the tray of overspilling silicone cups into the oven. She lowered her voice. 'But Jero's giving evidence at an important trial and there was no one to watch Aayla.'

Silence.

Then, an incredulous snort. 'Honestly, Ivy, listen to yourself. She's not your child, and this Javier guy...'

'Jero!'

'Lives on an island. In South America.'

'I am aware of that.'

'And you have equally important things to consider back here! I just want the best for you,

Ivy. Have you really thought about what you're doing, or *not* doing…?'

Ivy held the phone away from her ear as Aayla walked back into the kitchen holding half of a crumbled plastic brick castle. 'Pluma crashed into it.' She sighed, as if it happened all the time. 'We must rebuild, Ivy.'

'You're right,' she agreed solemnly. 'We shall rebuild.'

Ivy told her mother she had to go, and hung up. For the next two hours, they burned a batch of cupcakes, made one quite excellent batch that she vowed they'd deliver to poor Nina, and tried not to let Etta Malone's authoritarian agenda pour cold water over her mood. OK, so yes, she had shut up about her upcoming flight the second Jero had mentioned Aayla needed a minder. *Sucker.* And she'd cancelled it in her head the second he'd suggested they might work something out, even though the clinic was playing on her mind—all the unfinished business still left to attend to. But he'd said what she'd been waiting to hear. Finally. What else was she supposed to do? She was in love. Bursting with it, for the first time in her whole life.

Now. In no way was she the perfect babysitter, as demonstrated by the layer of chocolate and feathers where the kitchen counter used to be, but…

'Ivy, pass me that tree!'

She forgot what she'd been thinking. Aayla's sticky fingers had created a sheen all over the brick castle but the look on her face, deep in concentration over their rebuild while Pluma waddled about the living room, was priceless. What was a few more days here, in the grand scheme of things? She'd take a few more days when Jero returned, to iron out the details of his visit to Galway, and the possibility that she might come back here to be with him in the Galapagos. She had plenty of time to talk to Mike and the stuffy men from the Blue Stream Veterinary Alliance—life wasn't all work, work, work!

She paused, letting Aayla stop her from placing a tree on top of a castle turret, where it clearly did not belong.

Life wasn't all work, work, work.

She'd never let a thought like that cross her mind until now.

Day two of babysitting and, Ivy had to admit, she was pretty tired. The day had been jam-packed and she'd even had a visit by a mother from Aayla's school, along with three more six-year-olds. She didn't mind—exactly—but the hair-braiding session that had commenced had eaten into her scheduled call with Mike, till she'd had to postpone it altogether. She was almost asleep on the sofa when Jero called.

'How's the trial going? Are they going behind bars for life?' she asked as his handsome face beamed at her in the video-chat window. She was surprised to find butterflies in her belly as he told her all about it, and pride rushed through her, thinking of him standing up on behalf of the community. But she couldn't wait to get him back here.

'I'm missing you and Aayla,' he said. 'Are you having fun?'

'We sure are,' she replied, thinking it best not to say how exhausted she was. She recounted the trip to the shops, and the book they'd been reading on Irish folklore, but she omitted the guilt trip from her mother, which she'd been trying to forget about.

It wasn't easy. Her mother had a habit of getting under her skin.

'Hailey sent an email from New Zealand,' she remembered now. The first full-time surgeon Jero had had on his books for a while had called in to announce she wouldn't be coming back, which seemed to disappoint him. For a moment she wondered whether she should offer to take her place permanently, but something stopped her. She hadn't even spoken to Mike yet; she was rushing into things.

'Daddy!' Aayla interrupted, leaping in front of her, and she hurried a goodbye, and left them to talk, wishing she weren't suffering such a conflict of emotion. He wanted her here, she knew that now, he wanted to make things work, and so did she...but then again, what if she wasn't what they needed?

An hour later, she'd just sat down to check her emails and finally call Mike back when something huge clattered and thudded to the floor upstairs. Tossing her laptop aside, she sent Jero's guitar crashing to the floor, then raced up to Aayla's room with a pounding heart.

She threw the door open. 'What's wrong?'

Then she saw the dresser on its side and her heart all but stopped. 'Aayla?' One of the drawers had been pulled out and was smashed into a thousand splintered pieces on the carpet.

'I was standing on it,' she admitted sheepishly from the bed, where she was nursing a ginger kitten that she'd picked up from the clinic. Another animal who'd adopted Aayla more than the other way round. 'Lola was up on the curtain rails. Daddy doesn't like it when the animals climb the curtains.'

It took almost an hour for Ivy to sweep up all the pieces of the splintered drawer, and right the dresser. Now she'd have to report this damage to Jero and the thought of his disappointment made her cringe. She should have been watching her more carefully! What if Aayla had been squished under the dresser? It didn't bear thinking about.

Story time was next. She had to finish the book they'd started the night before, and by the time she got downstairs to check her email, she cursed herself at the significant chip on the neck of Jero's guitar.

To hell with emails, they could wait, she was too tired. Ivy poured herself a glass of wine, removed the braids from her hair, and vowed that tomorrow she'd be a shining example of authority and productivity.

That same night, halfway through a TV show about the mating cycle of penguins, she spotted a suspicious Manila file sticking out from under a pile of books on the shelf below the coffee table. She tried to straighten it up—symmetry was everything after all, not that Zenon's tattooist would agree—but then she spotted the words 'renovation plans' on the front, and she couldn't help a peek.

So, Jero had plans, it turned out. Plans to redesign the clinic! She studied them, impressed, and a little awed. It was clear from the apartment buildings that he had money in assets and, despite his humble lifestyle, he had plans to make use of that fact someday, for the good of the island, and the community.

That was so Jero.

The redesign went beyond anything she'd imagined, including open-air kennels with remote-controlled ceilings in case of rain, and a separate outhouse for storage and mobile-clinic supplies. He'd never mentioned wanting to redesign. But he was always so busy with things as they were now. Plus, he always seemed so reluctant to change!

Maybe he was waiting for the right time…or the right *person* to encourage him, she mused.

Day three of babysitting. Mike was in her ear now, and not just about the guys at Blue Stream Veterinary Alliance. He was asking her when she was coming home, and he had decidedly fewer nuggets of spiritual wisdom to impart this time. She was annoyed with herself for letting him down, and she told him so. He just sighed.

'I just didn't think you'd stay *this* long. Business aside, you know I want the best for you,' he said, in the strangest echo of her mother two days before. 'But you're not exactly the maternal type, are you, Ivy? I thought you didn't even want children.'

'She's not my child,' she heard herself say. But the very words from her mouth made her feel quite sick; Aayla felt unwanted enough by her own mother. Thank God she was dancing around the kitchen to Irish folk by The Dubliners—her new favourite—and hadn't heard. She lowered her voice. 'Anyway, why can't I change my mind?'

Mike stuttered a moment. 'Well…that would be great, good for you.'

He doesn't sound convinced, she thought. *He sounds like he thinks I'm losing the plot. Am I losing the plot?*

No…don't let him get in your head. Or your mother. Or yourself for that matter. Maybe you should meditate?

No time for that. Aayla was vying for her full attention again, this time with a dance performance. Ivy pulled her legs up under her on the familiar sofa and tried to ignore her calling laptop, and the chipped guitar.

Just focusing on Aayla's joy, with Pluma and her new stray kitten, Lola, as sidekicks quickly blocked everything out. The kid looked a picture with the hairstyle she'd given her. Ivy got to her knees and snapped a hundred photos with Aayla's new camera, in a hundred different exciting angles that made Aayla shriek in delight at having her own star gig photographer. The camera was the old one she'd asked Mike to post to the clinic; it had finally arrived.

In moments like this, she forgot everything else in the world, but in Jero's bed alone in the dark, she suffered through fevered dreams of missing planes and dodging falling furniture or sleeping in late from exhaustion and missing her shift. She couldn't let Jero or Aayla down. They'd been through so much. And she couldn't do this to Mike—he needed her. The guilt was insufferable. Old insecurities kept piling up like Lego bricks.

She was terrible at multitasking, she just wasn't equipped... She'd been trying to prove something to Jero because she was falling in love with him, but this wasn't her world and she'd never be good enough for him, or this little girl.

What was she *doing*?

CHAPTER SEVENTEEN

THE HOUSE WAS empty when Jero stepped inside. Tossing his keys onto the table, he called for Ivy and Aayla. No answer. He sprinted upstairs, thinking maybe he'd surprise them and walk in on them playing a game or something. Then he saw the smashed-up dresser. Frowning to himself, he scraped a hand over his head—what happened there? Where were they?

He grabbed his bicycle and found them both several minutes later, at the clinic. Dudders and Zenon greeted him with high-fives and Aayla rushed from the storeroom to hug him, abandoning the litter of kittens she was playing with, save for a ginger one that clung to her shoulder like a fuzzy accessory. Ivy pressed her back to the wall in Reception and started unbuttoning her white coat.

'Why didn't you tell me you were here?' He went to kiss her, but something wasn't right. Instincts primed, he took a step back. Her face

was a picture of concern in the light from a
small lamp shining onto an aquarium with a lizard in it. A tangle of cables was wrapped around
the tank, which annoyed him, but he couldn't
exactly fix it now.

'It was an emergency, another amputation,'
Ivy said, gesturing to a cage with a black puppy
in it. One hind leg was bandaged, the other missing. 'Good to have you back.'

Then she tossed her coat to the basket and pulled
Aayla into a huge embrace that both warmed his
heart and sent a chill straight through him.

'I have to go,' she announced to Aayla, smoothing down her hair. Aayla had the strangest hairstyle he'd ever seen, all backcombed like an
eighties singer. 'It was so much fun hanging out
with you!'

Aayla hugged her, as if she'd known this was
going to happen. 'Bye, Ivy!'

'Bye Ivy? Where are you going?'

'To the airport.'

Jero's heart kicked up a storm and thundered
in his chest. Ivy threw him a look he didn't like
one bit before making for the door.

'Guys, watch Aayla for me, please,' he said,
and followed her outside.

The taxi was waiting down the street. Ivy hurried across the gravel towards it, red hair fly-

ing. He called out to her, but she didn't answer. Without looking back, she yanked the door open urgently and climbed inside.

What the...?

Jero sprinted back for the bicycle and sped after the cab. The sun was starting to sink behind the trees and anger prickled his arms like mosquitoes. She was leaving now? Without so much as a goodbye?

He sped up and veered into a narrow lane that he knew would come out right in the taxi's path. Swerving in front of the car, he held his hand up, blinded by the lights. The driver skidded to a halt right in front of him, sending a shower of gravel into the air.

Jero tossed the bike aside and flung the taxi door open. 'What are you doing?'

Ivy squared her shoulders at him in the back seat, but her tears defied the fierce look on her face.

'I thought I'd save us both a goodbye, Jero. I can't pretend this is my life any more.'

'Get out of the car.'

She shook her head. His eyes found the bags piled up next to her; the stupid boots she'd arrived here in and tried to leave in before. 'Not this time,' she said. 'I have to go. I'm sorry, Jero, it's better this way. My flight leaves in two hours. I should have left ages ago.'

He bit his tongue. He should have seen it coming.

You are a total idiot, Jero!

She was leaving the second he'd relieved her of her babysitting duties!

Ivy liked Aayla enough, but she'd only been helping him out because of this little 'thing' between them. Now she'd had a taster of his real life and she was done.

He glowered at her, seeing red.

'How could you do this?' he hissed, gripping the top of the door, turning his knuckles white. He was about to tell her how much he'd trusted her, with himself, with Aayla, but the words were too humiliating to even say out loud. Why had he even let her in, and let himself fall for her?

'I'll pay for the damage to the dresser. And your guitar.'

My guitar, too?

'That's not what I'm talking about! I was falling in *love* with you.'

Ivy's eyes widened.

Jero faltered. Did he just say that out loud?

Ivy just sat there, rooted like a leaden weight, clutching her bag. She couldn't wait to go. The driver cleared his throat. It was all he could do not to kick something.

'Ivy, talk to me.'

Ivy squeezed her eyes shut and, this time, he did kick something—the tyre. The driver told him to back off and he apologised. This was all his fault. He'd let her in, fallen for her, even made tentative plans for a *future* when he should have known better. Hadn't he learned anything? They all left…all the tourists. He knew it and he'd dived right in again anyway and taken Aayla down with him.

'I'm sorry, Jero,' she sobbed, making to reach for him, but he moved from her grasp, gathering the strength he needed not to break something next. He'd already snapped, he had to cool it.

Before he could get his thoughts in order the taxi rumbled off, and he stood there in the fading light, shaken and fuming, willing himself not to go after her.

This wasn't some lame movie; *this* was how it ended.

Ivy heard the explosion as they reached the town borders. She almost hit her head on the car ceiling as the driver swerved to a stop again. What the hell was that?

Glancing behind her, she swiped at her wet eyes and tried to make sense of the tower of flames she could see, roaring out from behind the tree line.

The driver was talking fast in Spanish, asking

if she wanted to keep going towards the ferry, but now she could hear screams. Oh, God. Each one froze a little more of her blood. People were running out of their homes. Panic consumed her as grey smoke clouded the horizon. It was coming from the direction of the town, and the clinic.

'We have to go back!'

In seconds they were speeding back the way they came. Her brain was a cyclone tearing through horrific possibilities. The driver's radio buzzed, and she almost threw up as she recognised words: *Darwin Clinic. Fire brigade. People inside.*

No!

'Hurry!' she yelled. 'I'm a trained medic! What if there are injured animals?'

What if there are injured people?

Aayla was in there. Dudders and Zenon. Jero must have been on his way back…after she'd left him there, reeling.

No…

Ivy felt sick to the core as the driver put his foot down harder. Jero's face flashed into her mind…the look he'd given her when she'd told him she was on her way out, without even saying goodbye. He'd been falling in love with her. He'd said it. She'd almost got out of the car to say it back, but she hadn't.

Why hadn't she? *Coward.* 'Hurry up, please,' she urged again in Spanish.

All this time she'd told herself he was in it for some fun with a tourist, but it had meant just as much to him as her. And she'd hit him where it hurt: straight in his own fear of abandonment by someone else he trusted.

She was just scared of him loving her, she realised, almost as much as having no one love her at all. She was scared of loving anyone that hard, in case they left her; in case they decided at any point that she was merely just getting in the way of something better. It was always there in the back of her mind. Jero had told her she was enough, already, and she hadn't let herself believe it.

A siren blared in the distance as they swung onto the street where they'd started, metres from the clinic. It just didn't feel or look like the same place. Heavy noxious smoke formed an ominous wall, blocking her vision. Leaping from the cab, she made for the clinic—or the place where the clinic used to be. The fire seemed to be raging out of control.

For a second she was shocked still in a whirl of smoke and heat and ashes. Everything was burning. Everything he'd worked for. She gasped at the towering flames licking the roof, devouring the walls. Behind her the driver yelled at her to turn back, but no...*no way*. Aayla was in there!

'Jero!' she yelled. 'Aayla!'

Dudders was behind her now. He grabbed at her arm and made to pull her back, and to her utter relief she saw Zenon holding Aayla to him, metres away by the trees.

'Aayla,' she called, racing over to her through the smoke. She coughed and almost had to stop halfway but Aayla's arms locked around her middle like a baby octopus and Ivy drew strength from nowhere, scooped her up in her arms. 'You're OK, you're OK...'

'I'm OK, but Daddy's inside!' Aayla wailed against her, louder than the sirens, and Ivy somehow made it to the guys and their open arms, fighting for words and her own breath.

'Jero went in there?'

'He went to get the kittens,' Dudders stammered, his face lit up by the orange inferno. Ashes smouldered in his dreadlocks. The black dog in the cage sat at his feet, and more people were gathering on the periphery by the minute, watching in shock and fear, and tears. Some were throwing water feebly at the flames from plastic bottles.

Through her panic Ivy mentally tried to recount which other animals had been inside, but Jero...oh, God, what had possessed him to go in there? And where was the fire brigade? Why were things always so slow around here?!

'Daddy!' Aayla fought her way from her arms and Ivy blinked in disbelief, just as the crowd started buzzing and cheering.

'What the…?' Ivy squinted into the smoke where the entrance would usually be, and then she saw him.

A huge sob that had been building in her throat almost threatened to topple her. Jero staggered into the light, silhouetted by the blaze. He was holding a box of squirming kittens. His clothes were blackened, his skin ashen grey. He had never looked better. *Thank God, you're alive!*

Running towards him, she was blocked in her tracks by a crew of paramedics who'd somehow arrived on the scene with the fire engine while she'd been fixated on Jero emerging from the building. Ivy was forced to watch it all from the sidelines like a dream as he was wrapped in a blanket without so much as noticing her and ushered into the ambulance with Aayla.

She had no choice but to watch it roll away, while she stood there between Zenon and Dudders, witnessing Jero's empire burn to the ground. The firefighters couldn't save it. Within the hour, the Darwin Clinic was nothing but a pile of rubble and smouldering ashes and all she could think was, thank the heavens and all the angels in the sky that he hadn't been burnt to a crisp along with it.

She couldn't lose him, as her mother had lost her dad. She knew that now; she'd known it the second he'd told her he was falling in love with her, too. He might just be the love of her life.

CHAPTER EIGHTEEN

JERO'S THROAT FELT as if he'd swallowed jet fuel.
The hospital room seemed to swim around him
as the nurse left. He could barely speak or swallow, and he wanted nothing more than to go
home.

He clenched his fists, willing the hellish imag-
ery of the evening to leave him. First, Ivy, all but
running for that taxicab, away from him. Then
the clinic going up in flames. He'd seen his life
flash before his eyes the second the glass shat-
tered in the front windows, right as he'd made
it back to the forecourt.

'Can I come in?' Ivy asked from the doorway, making his head turn, and his pulse spike.
Every muscle in his body had just tensed up, as
if she'd walked in with a cattle prod.

'I thought you'd be halfway to Galway by
now,' he managed as she pulled up a seat by
the bed.

'Well, surprise, the explosion made me turn around.'

At first his defences were primed. Then he softened in her gaze, as he always did. Already he adored every angle and line of her face. He liked it so much that sometimes even looking at her caused a strange, aching sensation around his heart, in his chest and in his throat and he'd thought about her the entire time he'd been away. Even if this was yet another temporary delay before she left—again—she was impossible to be mad at.

'I'm so sorry, Jero. The whole clinic…it's gone.' She put two hands to his arm, one over his tattoo, and her warmth softened him even more. He must be a total sucker because he was glad, in this moment, that she was here. Almost as glad as he was to still be here.

Zenon and Dudders had somehow made it out with the dog, but he'd had to go back in for the kittens. No animal was going to perish if he could help it, not on his watch. The heat had been suffocating. He'd had to crawl on his hands and knees just to see in front of him, across the piles of blazing Manila folders and melting wall panels. He'd thought of Ivy in there. Wondered for a moment if their angry exchange would be the last thing she'd remember of him.

'Yes, it's gone, but no one died,' he said, aware it sounded too flippant for the severity of the situation but what was he supposed to do? Cry about it? He'd move on, as he'd had to do before. 'What made you come back?'

'Jero, even before the clinic went up in flames, I knew I'd messed up.' Her voice sounded choked now. 'I shouldn't have tried to go without talking to you. I was just afraid of how I'd started to feel about you, and Aayla. I'm not used to this…' She gestured between them, as if there were some invisible forcefield she didn't know how to turn off. He bit into his cheeks.

'Neither am I,' he said stiffly, and she leaned in, pressed a hand to his cheek the way she did.

'I know you trusted me.'

'I shouldn't have been so angry…'

'I wrecked the house, your dresser, your guitar, I am a rubbish babysitter.'

He stared at her, not sure what to say. Did she really think he cared about material objects more than people, and animals, and her? He hadn't seen the guitar yet, but it couldn't be as bad as the pile of rubble that now constituted the Darwin Clinic.

'I was just convinced I was no good for you, no good with kids. It doesn't mean I don't love them or want them in my life. Maybe I do. I think I probably do.' She squeezed his arm earnestly and he almost smiled.

'I want you and Aayla in my life,' she clarified quickly. 'If you'll still have me, if you meant what you said, maybe we can work something out. You could come to Ireland while the clinic's being rebuilt?'

He laughed to himself under his breath, then coughed again. Ivy looked hurt as she passed him some water, and he shook his head. 'No, no, I like that idea,' he said, taking a huge gulp from the glass. The idea started to take shape in his mind, and slowly it pushed some of the horrors of the night aside. Galway with Ivy… Aayla would lose her mind.

'But we can't rebuild so easily. There's no insurance, for a start.'

Ivy's eyes grew round. She sat back in her seat and dragged a hand through her hair.

'It was built on community funding…every cent went back into supplies. We just never thought we'd need it. I can sell some of my properties, I guess… I have assets.'

He knew what she was thinking. You could never run a clinic in the western world without insurance, but that wasn't exactly the case out here. That place had started life as a shack and treatments were free.

He didn't even want to think about it now. He

took her hands in his and brought them to his lips. Everything ached, even his eyes, but somehow the monster started to shift on his chest, till he barely felt its weight.

'We shall rebuild,' Ivy said thoughtfully, almost to herself, tightening her hands around his. A small smile lit up her impish eyes as they locked onto his again. He didn't even have a chance to ask what she was talking about before she leaned across the bed and pressed her lips to his.

'I'm in love with you too,' she said, against his mouth, drawing him closer by the scruff of his blackened shirt and kissing him more passionately than he'd ever been kissed in a hospital bed...right until another knock on the door forced them apart.

Dudders looked at them, his face reddening.

'It's OK, you can come in,' Jero said, still clutching Ivy's hand to his heart. She perched on the bed next to him.

'How are you feeling?' Dudders asked him, stopping by the bedside in another pair of Thai fisherman pants and placing some scrawny yellow flowers wrapped in cellophane on the bedside cabinet.

'Alive. What happened?' he asked now, annoyed at the croak that came out instead. 'What started the fire, do we know yet?'

Dudders looked sideways. 'The fire marshal thinks it was a faulty plug,' he admitted with a wince.

Instantly Jero recalled the wires and cables he'd seen wrapped around the aquarium, where a lizard had been lounging under a lamp. That poor lizard probably didn't make it.

'Ivy told me to ask you how old the extension lead was, but you were busy...' Dudders trailed off, fumbling with his dreadlocks. 'It's no excuse, I totally forgot. I just plugged it in anyway and went back to work.'

'That thing was at least a decade old.' Jero sighed. 'It's not your fault.'

It wasn't, really, they'd all made mistakes with that place. Ivy squeezed his hand reassuringly. 'Ivy was the only one who's tried to make a difference in ages,' he said, to her more than Dudders. 'We should've been more grateful. At least, thanks to you, Ivy, we didn't lose all our data.'

'You need to rest, stop talking,' Ivy instructed now, and his mind churned while the two of them discussed rehoming the animals. What a relief she'd been so adamant about setting up the database. Ivy had technically, or technologically, he supposed, saved the clinic from total destruction. Despite his plans to renovate and remodel he'd let the usual daily grind consume him, till it had all taken a back seat. Those damn plans had been sitting there for months under the coffee table, maybe even years, but he hadn't found the time to act on them. He hadn't even told Ivy he'd met with a design team; she would have tried to push him to do things better, as she always did. Which wasn't a bad thing at all. It was what he needed.

'There's no point beating yourself up over it, Jero,' Ivy said when Dudders left. She knew, clearly, that he was mulling over his mistakes right now.

She leaned in and kissed him again, emptying his head of everything but her as he responded on autopilot, as magnetic as she was. It was no good, getting a hard-on in a hospital bed, but to hell with it. He threw the blankets aside and she scrambled up to the bed, wrapping her arms around him. It was way too small for both of them, and the nurse looked at them in vague disapproval on her way past, but he didn't care. They slept that way all night, his fingers tangled in her hair, her legs entwined with his, and in the morning, Ivy took him home.

EPILOGUE

Eight months later

Ivy STUDIED THE new giant bronze statue of Pluma in flight on the Darwin Clinic's new paved forecourt. Aayla had suggested it, the way a six-year-old might also suggest building a pink candyfloss castle in the surrounding trees, but Jero had taken it quite seriously. He'd commissioned an artist from Quito and now it made quite the eye-catching mascot.

Right now, the site was bustling with construction workers, and the electrician was thankfully ensuring there were more than enough electrical outlets to handle everything they might need to plug in. Goosebumps prickled up and down her spine every time they were on site. She had a new baby now—one with Jero.

'Not long to go,' Jero said, walking up behind them. He was carrying a huge potted palm. She jumped up to help him, just as Zenon intervened and took it from his hands.

'Let me, boss,' he said, and he proceeded to struggle with it all the way to the entrance. She bit back a smile. He was doing his best.

'How are my girls?' Jero asked, planting a kiss on her forehead, then another onto Aayla's. He had mud on his face from the trip to the garden centre, and she wiped it off with her finger. He caught her hand and kissed her, and she smiled at the *Who's Your Paddy?* shirt he was wearing; the one he'd thought was hilarious and had picked up in Galway on their trip.

It was crazy the way her heart still jolted in her chest every time he made an appearance. He dropped to the low brick wall and took her hand, watching Zenon place the giant plant down.

She and Jero had worked with an architect and interior designer to take his plans—the ones she didn't think necessary to tell him she'd discovered ages ago—to new heights. They were creating the most perfect space with two consultation rooms, a spacious operating room, plenty of storage and a fully functioning kennel with a remote-controlled ceiling cover for rainy days.

Aayla had chosen seven very specific photos of her favourite animals, all snapped by herself, of course. And why not? She was very talented. They were set to be displayed in frames for all to see, the second their clients walked in. No more drooping posters. No more laptop either, and definitely no more Manila folders.

The morning of the launch Ivy slipped into a new emerald-green floor-length dress and called for Jero to help her zip it up. He didn't answer.

'Aayla,' she called down the stairs. 'Where's your dad?'

'He went out already,' she called back from the kitchen.

Ivy frowned to herself. They were supposed to have been walking down there together, but maybe there was some kind of problem. He could have been called out while she was in the shower, she supposed.

Taking a deep breath and spritzing herself with perfume, she tried not to think that anything was wrong. Whenever he went somewhere and didn't tell her, the old insecurities crept back in…but she channelled Mike and his Oprah quotes, and envisaged her demons being swept into the abyss on the back of a giant flying whale.

Just because her father had gone out one day and never come home didn't mean anything was wrong with Jero. Besides, he was a survivor, just ask the kittens he'd saved by walking into a burning building, she thought with fresh pride.

'We need to go!' Aayla called now, stopping her from trying to call Jero anyway. 'Daddy will meet us there.'

'He'd better,' she mumbled to herself, pinning the golden bird-shaped clip in her hair and taking one last look in the mirror. She looked good, like a head veterinarian in the Galapagos should look, minus the white coat and cat scratches, she decided.

The second she hit the Darwin Clinic's forecourt with Aayla, she could tell something was up. 'What are all these people doing here…?' She trailed off as she spotted Mike, over by the giant Pluma statue. 'Mike?'

Was she imagining things? What the heck was Mike doing here? Adrenaline flooded her veins. Then, she spotted her mother. Etta Malone looked slightly overwhelmed in a fitted pinstriped suit, fanning her face against the heat. Ivy blinked.

What the…?

'There you are!' She barely noticed Jero walking up to her, but he led her in a daze into the crowd, where her mother embraced her and kissed her on both cheeks.

'Hello, darling.'

She lowered herself to Aayla's level. 'Hello

again, you. Have you grown since I saw you in Ireland?'

'At least an inch,' Aayla responded proudly, just as Pluma decided to try and perch on Ivy's mother's shoulder. Etta let out the hugest shriek Ivy had ever heard, making Pluma flap her giant wings above her head. The motions sent her mother's red hair in a thousand directions, but as laughter erupted around them Etta saw the funny side, thank goodness.

'You weren't kidding about this thing,' she said, eyeing Pluma warily as the bird settled on one of the statue's outstretched wings.

'What's going on?' Ivy was almost too stunned by all this to construct a sentence. She flicked her gaze from her mother to Jero, but Mike was engulfing her now, in the hugest hug he'd ever given her.

'The place looks incredible, Ivy, congrats. And this island... wow. Now I see why you wanted to stay so much. If I'd come here on holiday I might not have left either.'

Her mother nudged him and smiled sideways. 'I don't think it was just the clinic that attracted her,' she said. They both turned their gaze to Jero, who was now lifting Aayla up onto his shoulders to place a crown of flowers on the giant booby statue's head.

Someone handed him a microphone. Everyone cried out 'speech', and he lowered Aayla to the ground and got up onto the stage. Jero was wearing real shoes for once, a crisp designer shirt and jeans. He was impossibly handsome, not to mention devious, she thought, still dazed. How the heck had he managed to arrange for her mother, and Mike to both be here for the opening without her finding out?

She was surprised either one of them had come; they were both so busy. Although admittedly Mike was busy vacationing with his family. He'd decided to take some well-deserved time off after they'd sold the clinic.

Maybe, just like her, her mother had put work aside for a while, too. She couldn't wait to show them both the other islands, the albatross chicks, Álvaro…

Álvaro?

The crowd erupted into gasps and laughter again and Ivy felt herself being ushered forwards, her mother and Mike on either arm. The giant sea lion had waddled in from the sidelines with Marsha. Ivy watched in amazement as he hopped on his fins right up the steps, onto the stage.

Jero placed the mic in front of him and he honked on cue, making Etta jump and smooth down her suit self-consciously. Ivy felt a rush of warmth for her. She was probably embarrassed to be seen so out of her comfort zone, and being Irish she wasn't used to the heat, but she'd come. She'd made an effort.

'I had no idea he was doing this…' she started as Jero called her up on stage. Nerves gripped her as she climbed the steps. It felt so strange, seeing everyone's eyes on her.

Jero took her hand. 'I'd like to thank everyone for coming here, to the reopening of the Darwin Clinic,' he said into the mic. 'I wouldn't have been able to do this without Ivy Malone.'

'Well, I wouldn't have been able to do it without you,' she added, over the cheers and whoops and claps. They were equal partners, after all. She'd invested in the Darwin Clinic with funding from her clinic's acquisition. At first Jero had been reluctant to agree; he had the funds tied up in assets, and community drives would raise more cash in no time, but to Ivy it wasn't about that.

She wanted to contribute something more meaningful to a community, to the Galapagos eco-system, something that made a difference. And she wanted to do it with him.

Her mother winked at her now, and Ivy bit back a smile.

'What do you think about it, Álvaro?' Jero asked.

At that, Álvaro rose high onto his hind fins and batted his front fins together. Her jaw dropped. 'How did you…?'

Had the wild creature they'd rescued been getting lessons from some kind of Galapagos ringmaster?

Everyone went wild again, and she turned to Jero, only to see it was Marsha giving the creature a secret set of instructions. She must have been teaching him. *Incredible.* She was just about to say that they had a brand-new tourist attraction for the market now, when she caught Marsha placing something into Álvaro's front fins.

A small red box.

Her heart catapulted straight out of her body and back again. In the crowd, her mother's eyes were glistening. Mike was grinning like the Cheshire Cat. Did they know this was going to happen? Time seemed to slow right down as Jero got to one knee on the stage.

'Ivy…' He trailed off, grinning as the crowd started buzzing with excitement. Ivy felt hot, her green dress was sticking to her already, she wasn't prepared for this…hadn't been expecting this at all. Was he serious?

Now?

In front of all these people?

Oh, my God.

Jero cleared his throat, scanned her eyes as if asking if she was OK. Instantly, with that one look, she calmed down. She was OK. She was more than OK.

Jero looked more serious than she'd ever seen him. 'Ivy. I can't imagine doing this with anyone else. You've changed my life. Will you do me the incredible honour of starting this new chapter as my wife? Will you marry me?'

'Yes.' She whispered it at first. She was still shaking. Then the nervous laughter crept in. 'Yes,' she repeated, louder, into the microphone. 'Yes, Jero, I will marry you!'

Somewhere in the crowd she heard Dudders emit a wolf whistle that could have summoned every dog on the island.

Aayla jumped up and down, clapping her hands together along with Álvaro. Pluma flapped around their heads, as if she were congratulating them too, and Marsha leaned in to hug them both at the same time. Ivy found Jero's eyes amid the chaos and told him without even moving her mouth how much she loved him.

This was, quite possibly, the best day, no, *year* of her life, she decided.

When they finally got a moment alone, she poured all her love into her kisses and tried not to cry. There was so much to look forward to, so many more creatures to care for, so many things to get done…but for now, she decided, she would enjoy her life, moment by moment.

* * * * *

*If you enjoyed this story, check out
these other great reads from
Becky Wicks*

A Princess in Naples
White Christmas with Her Millionaire Doc
Fling with the Children's Heart Doctor
Falling Again for the Animal Whisperer

All available now!